Apparently the infamous Luca Petrelli had dragged himself away from the French Riviera and the parties in Rio de Janeiro. Enter one recalcitrant playboy who flaunted his charms from one end of the globe to another.

Charli stopped outside the suite and knocked, quickly relaxing her face into neutral. This was a job, just like any other, and she had no right to second-guess her boss.

However, as the door swung open and she caught her first glimpse of Luca Petrelli, she knew this was no ordinary job.

"You look disappointed," he drawled, holding the door open with one hand, leaning against the jamb with the other, naked from the waist up.

She didn't dare glance down to assess the rest of the situation, though as a jumble of emotions tumbled through Charli disappointment wasn't one of them.

Heat surged to her cheeks, scorching a few choice parts in her body along the way, and she focused on his face.

Bad move.

The body was bad enough. Combined with the slashed cheekbones, cut jaw and dark blue eyes the color of Melbourne's night sky, the guy should be branded illegal.

NICOLA MARSH has always had a passion for writing and reading. As a youngster, she devoured books when she should have been sleeping, and later kept a diary whose content could be an epic in itself! These days, when she's not enjoying life with her husband and son in her home city of Melbourne, she's at her computer, creating the romances she loves, in her dream job. Visit Nicola's website at www.nicolamarsh.com for the latest news of her books.

Books by Nicola Marsh

Harlequin Presents® EXTRA
151—HER BAD, BAD BOSS
107—OVERTIME IN THE BOSS'S BED

SEX, GOSSIP AND ROCK & ROLL

NICOLA MARSH

~ Tabloid Scandals ~

Harlequin®

TORONTO NEW YORK LONDON
AMSTERDAM PARIS SYDNEY HAMBURG
STOCKHOLM ATHENS TOKYO MILAN MADRID
PRAGUE WARSAW BUDAPEST AUCKLAND

Recycling programs
for this product may
not exist in your area.

ISBN-13: 978-0-373-52836-3

SEX, GOSSIP AND ROCK & ROLL

First North American Publication 2011

SEX, GOSSIP AND
ROCK & ROLL

This one's for the lovely Natalie Anderson,
who was my rock throughout the writing
of this book.

Thanks, Nat, for the cyber chats,
hugs and general championing. We'll catch
up for that coffee one day, promise!

CHAPTER ONE

CHARLI loathed babysitting.

Not that she had anything against kids, per se, but having her boss's grandson tag along on Storm Varth's comeback tour sucked.

Big-time.

As if minding the wild rock star wasn't bad enough, she had to worry about Luca Petrelli watching her every move.

Not good.

Stabbing at the elevator button, she glanced around the lobby of Melbourne's Crown Towers, the familiar muted golds and warm browns exuding class and sophistication.

She practically lived in this hotel with the number of international musos and rock stars that stayed here. And where Landry Records stars stayed, she'd be there, catering to their every whim.

It was what she did best: pamper visiting rock royalty, arrange VIP services, guarantee every second of every itinerary ran like clockwork.

She thrived on it; the buzz, the rush, the pressure of ensuring the plans she put into place ran smoothly.

Nothing fazed her. Not any more.

Stepping into the elevator, she glanced at her watch

and grimaced. Luca Petrelli had better be ready and waiting when she knocked on his door, or else.

She'd co-ordinated their departure and arrival time between here and Ballarat to the last second. Storm's tour bus had just taken off and while the surly rock star had demanded he not be approached until morning, she wanted to ensure his arrival at the first stop of his tour of Victoria went off without a hitch.

She had things to do and no one, not even some notorious slack-arse playboy, would slow her down.

As the elevator doors soundlessly slid open, she smoothed down her favourite aubergine skirt, adjusted her jacket and stepped out, a quick glance at the numbers on the wall sending her right.

She marched up the long corridor, her impatience growing with every step.

She'd do anything for Hector Landry, CEO of Australia's biggest recording label, but when her boss and mentor had sprung the surprise of Luca's unwelcome presence on her a few hours ago, she'd almost balked.

Okay, so she'd been a little harsh in labelling his presence *babysitting some idle playboy*. Apparently the infamous Luca Petrelli had dragged himself away from the French Riviera and the parties in Rio de Janeiro as a favour to Hector, who'd just fired his top financier and needed a quickie replacement on this tour.

Enter one recalcitrant playboy who flaunted his charms from one end of the globe to another. The fact he used his public profile to raise money for charities only served to raise her suspicions.

If the guy hadn't been near his grandfather in the past ten years, what the hell was he doing here now?

She stopped outside the suite and knocked, quickly relaxing her face into neutral. This was a job, just like any other she'd done for Hector and she had no right to second-guess her boss or the rationale behind his flaky grandson's visit.

However, as the door swung open and she caught her first glimpse of Luca Petrelli, she knew this was no ordinary job.

'You look disappointed,' he drawled, holding the door open with one hand, leaning against the jamb with the other, naked from the waist up.

She didn't dare glance down to assess the rest of the situation, though as a jumble of emotions tumbled through Charli disappointment wasn't one of them.

She'd seen pictures of Luca in magazines, taking time to politely glance at the odd snapshot Hector would point out to her. The pride in Hector's voice had always grated. How could he be proud of a layabout grandson who never visited let alone acknowledged he existed?

So while she'd glanced at those pictures she'd never really looked at them, had the impression of a tallish guy with too-long hair, too much stubble and too many bimbos.

The reality was far different.

He'd cut his hair, dark caramel curls spiking in all directions, he'd shaved and there wasn't a busty Botoxed blonde in sight.

'Disappointed?' she managed to mutter when he cocked an eyebrow, her silence and none-too-subtle stares earning her a lazy grin. A lazy, *sexy* grin that made her whimper inside.

Hell.

'That I'm not a rock star.'

'No chance of confusing you for a rock star.'

Her gaze reluctantly dropped to his chest and she struggled not to gasp. Broad, bronze, beautifully sculpted, the guy was nothing like the emaciated, pale stars she routinely dealt with.

The rock stars she managed were nocturnal creatures, at ease in the darkness of smoky clubs and dark stages, chain-smoking to ease nerves, or worse.

No way could Luca Petrelli in all his six-four bronzeness be mistaken for a washed-out rocker.

Leaning against the door frame, he smiled, and she could've sworn the whimper turned to a roar.

'Why's that? Don't I look the part?'

Despite every self-preservation mechanism telling her not to look down, her gaze travelled from his chest lower and she exhaled in relief when she spied a towel. A towel loosely knotted in front. Where she might have glimpsed movement…

Heat surged to her cheeks, scorching a few choice parts in her body along the way, and she focused on his face.

Bad move.

The body was bad enough. Combined with the slashed cheekbones, cut jaw and dark blue eyes the colour of Melbourne's night sky, the guy should be branded illegal.

'Problem?'

Quelling the urge to turn and run, she frowned. 'You're not dressed.'

'You noticed.'

Her heart leaped at the wicked glint in his eyes and she slapped it down.

'Because if the towel's a problem, I could lose it—'

'I'll give you five minutes.'

'Or what?'

As he leaned forward a tantalising blend of expensive

toiletries and freshly showered male washed over her, undermining her anger.

The guy was a player. He flirted for a living. So why was she tempted to broach the short distance between them, bury her nose in the crook of his neck and inhale deeply?

'Just do it,' she said, annoyed by the slightest quiver in her voice. 'We have to hit the road.'

'Your loss.'

He shrugged and turned away as she gaped at his insolence. Not that it stopped her watching him stride across the room, the thick white bath sheet draped provocatively low on his hips, clinging to his butt with every tempting step.

The man was a menace.

Whatever she'd expected, this wasn't it.

Luca Petrelli in the flesh was a lot more disarming, a lot more charming, than she'd expected. And the fact she hadn't had a date in ages went a long way to explaining why her hormones were shimmying along behind him, tugging at that damn towel.

He paused at the bathroom door and she quickly glanced up. Not quick enough if his smug grin was any indication.

'You've misjudged me.'

'How's that?'

'You don't think I have what it takes to be a rock star?' He pointed to the towel and smirked. 'You should see my tat.'

In her imagination, her traitorous hormones couldn't rip the towel off him quick enough.

In reality, she turned her back on his chuckles and prayed for immunity against rogue playboy charmers.

CHAPTER TWO

LUCA whistled as he zipped his oldest jeans and shrugged into a black cashmere pullover, grinning at his reflection in the bathroom mirror.

By his reckoning, he had another three minutes before the fiery blonde pacing his suite barged in here and dragged him out.

She'd given him five minutes to get ready.

He'd deliberately taken ten.

Whatever he'd expected from Pop's PA, Charli Chambers wasn't it.

Sure, he'd been away awhile—give or take ten years—but Pop had always had sedate, subservient employees, women who wore bland grey trouser suits and conservative blouses. Stereotypical drones who wouldn't say boo to Australia's top musical entrepreneur.

Charli Chambers was far from stereotypical.

Her knee-length purple skirt hugged a butt made to be grabbed by a guy's hand, her fitted jacket outlined a hand-span waist and the deep V of her crisp white shirt highlighted a very nice cleavage indeed.

As for those long stockingless legs…shapely calves, trim ankles, manicured silver nails peeping from open-toe designer sandals… Yep, he was a leg man and proud of it.

But it wasn't her designer outfit or sexy shoes that surprised him as much as her lousy attitude. If her dismissive tone wasn't bad enough, she'd looked at him as if he'd stolen every one of her favourite CDs.

She didn't trust him.

He knew the look well: it was the same one he'd learned to hide from an early age, when he quickly learned you couldn't trust anyone, even so-called family.

The thing was, Charli shouldn't be looking at him with mistrust; it should be the other way around. He'd Googled Pop's protégé and what he'd found raised hackles of distrust.

He'd expected to find the odd mention of her in an occasional newspaper article linked to Pop. What he'd discovered was a plethora of pictures: Charli hanging off Pop's arm at some charity shindig, Charli dining with Pop at countless fund-raising balls, Charli accompanying Pop on his overseas jaunts.

Where Pop went, she shadowed and it immediately set his alarm bells ringing. He knew what it was like, having people fawn over him just because he had money, and if Charli thought she could take advantage of Pop...

His grin faded and he absent-mindedly rubbed his stomach at the sudden gripe. He might not be close to Pop but he owed him and if there was one thing he'd learned it was to pay his dues, and if that included protecting Pop from money-grabbers in designer PA clothing, so be it.

Pushing off the bathroom sink, he flung open the door.

He'd given Pop a fortnight. Two weeks to manage

Landry Records' finances of some over-the-hill rock star's tour before he headed back to London.

Before he did, he had every intention of sussing out Miss Snooty Britches.

Charli glanced at the gold Tag Heuer Hector had given her on her twenty-first for the fifth time in as many minutes, cursed under her breath and glared at the bathroom door, ready to kick it down.

She'd thought it might take a pampered playboy longer than the average guy to get ready but he'd been in there for ten freaking minutes! What was he doing? Plucking individual nose hairs?

Having Luca Petrelli tag along on this tour had been bad enough. Then he'd opened the door wearing that damn towel and her misgivings had shot into the stratosphere.

The guy was cocky, brash and annoying.

Don't forget hot, an annoying little voice in her head whispered, and she gritted her teeth.

As if she needed reminding. The image of that broad, tanned chest was imprinted on her brain like the passwords to all Hector's accounts.

And that was what had her mad as hell. His disregard for punctuality stung but the fact her skin prickled with heat every time she closed her eyes and saw his naked torso burned into her retinas? Now that seriously peed her off.

Clenching her fists, she marched towards the bathroom, raised a hand to thump on the door at the exact second it opened and she stumbled headlong into the chest she'd been fantasising about less than five seconds ago.

'Falling for me already?'

Luca's deep voice murmured in her ear but that wasn't what had her knees wobbling. Uh-uh, his hands grasping her wrists, pressing her palms against his chest, a chest radiating enough heat to warm the entire suite, took care of that.

'I'm flattered, but shouldn't we go through the motions first? A date? Dinner?'

'You wish.'

She pushed against his chest and he released her. She should've been glad but as she reluctantly dragged her gaze upwards to meet his, saw the spark of heat there, his regret matched hers.

The corners of his lips quirked into a decadent smile that must've slain females the world over—and had, if the glossies were to be believed.

'You have no idea what I wish for, Goldi.'

'It's Charli,' she snapped, angry at herself for being this close to him, for enjoying his banter, for her damn knees still wobbling courtesy of that smile. 'Where'd you get Goldi from?'

His patronising pat on the cheek had her fist clenching to slug him.

'It's an abbreviation.'

Confused, she glared at him. 'Short for what?'

'Gold-digger.'

Stupefied, her jaw dropped as he slung a Vuitton overnight bag over his shoulder and strutted out of the door.

Charli caught up with Luca at the lift, grabbing his bag so he had no option but to stop.

'What did you just call me?'

He'd lost the smile, the spark in his eyes replaced by suspicion.

'You heard me.'

Taking a deep breath, she mentally counted to five, a technique Hector had taught her when he'd first rescued her from the streets. Back then, she'd fly into a rage at the slightest provocation and, while she'd come a long way, having hotshot Luca Petrelli stare at her as if she'd pilfered his Rolex grated.

'You've got the wrong idea. I'm not here out of choice. I'm just doing my job.'

Confusion creased his brow for a moment before he laughed.

'You think I think you're after my money?'

Now it was her turn to be confused. 'Isn't that what you meant?'

'Nice try to deflect, Goldi, shame it didn't work.'

'Stop calling me that!'

'If the Louboutin fits.'

He dropped his gaze to her shoes, and she didn't know what unsettled her more. The fact he recognised the artistic brilliance of her favourite shoe designer or the way his gaze slowly travelled upwards the entire length of her leg, lingering along the way.

'If I'm not after your money, who...?' She trailed off, a nasty thought sliding insidiously into her brain.

He didn't speak, merely raised an eyebrow, as if taunting her to drop the act.

She'd drop something all right. Right onto his big fat mistaken head.

Beyond indignant she straightened, took two steps forwards until they were toe to toe, and eyeballed him.

'Not that I owe you anything, let alone an explanation, but Hector is my boss. I'm his executive assistant. We're friends and I'd never do anything to take advantage of that. So you can take your stupid misconceptions and stick them.'

Surprise widened his eyes before he blinked, studying her as if she were a clue to the missing link.

'So it's in your job description to accompany him to balls? Charity functions? That kind of thing?'

To her mortification she blushed, an annoying heat that flushed her cheeks and notched up her temper.

'My job description is none of your business.'

Charli had been called many things in her life, had shrugged off the nasty labels of spending part of her life on the streets. She'd heard the gossip about her relationship with Hector many times and had given it the attention drivel like that deserved: absolutely none.

Over the years she'd developed a thick skin from necessity. Nothing or no one could hurt her.

So why the hell was she fuming now, so furious she could strangle Luca, leave him slumped in the hallway and not look back?

'Fair call.'

His finger hovered over the elevator button, his smile as infuriating as the implication behind his accusation a few moments ago. 'You coming?'

'Not 'til you apologise for being so vile.'

His grin broadened and her hands clenched into fists. Just another step and she'd be close enough to slug him…

'Now, we both know that's a lie.'

She frowned, not following as he crowded her personal space but she didn't give an inch, wouldn't give him the satisfaction.

'What are you going on about?'

'You don't think I'm vile.'

He leaned close enough to murmur in her ear, close enough a wave of some expensive citrus aftershave washed over her, close enough for her to feel the heat radiating off him and she gritted her teeth against the impulse to get closer.

'Not by the way you were looking at me earlier in that towel.'

He popped the intimate bubble enveloping them just like that and she shoved him away.

Mistake number two: placing her palms on that hard chest again.

Mistake number one had happened the instant she'd agreed to have him tag along on this tour.

Taking a deep breath to steady her rampaging pulse, she pinned him with a glare he couldn't mistake for anything other than 'take one step closer to me again and you die'.

'I've changed my mind. You can shove your apology and your sexy smiles. Let's go.'

She stabbed at the elevator button and broke a nail in the process.

Thankfully, he kept his mouth shut. Until they stepped into the elevator and the doors slid soundlessly shut.

'So you think my smile's sexy, huh?'

Charli silently called herself some very unladylike names and clamped her lips shut in response.

Luca couldn't help himself. There was something delightfully alluring about a woman who didn't fall at his feet. Sure, he liked a challenge as much as the next guy, but lately even dating the newest Oscar winner or squiring a princess around Europe had lost its thrill.

He knew why he did it, of course, was well aware of how every paparazzi picture or each gossip-column mention vindicated the choices he'd made. Childish and puerile, maybe, but every time he saw himself in the press, he hoped the people who'd shunned him had their snooty noses rubbed in it.

As the valet steered a low-slung bright red Ferrari to stop in front of them he wolf-whistled.

'Some car.'

She shot him another death glare that did nothing but turn him on as she stepped around the bonnet and held out her hand to the valet.

The Ferrari was hers? Jeez, and he'd started to believe her story about not taking advantage of Pop. No way no how could an executive assistant afford a car like this.

She flashed the valet a glorious smile that only served to rile him further—he wouldn't mind being on the end of one of those—and slid into the car, her skirt riding mid-thigh, his libido shooting sky-high. Those long, gorgeous legs could be put to much better use than pushing pedals.

Easing his overnight bag into the back seat, he slid into the passenger side, admiring her driving skill as she guided the car out of Crown and into the heavy city traffic.

When she kept up the silent treatment for six blocks, he said, 'Nice wheels.'

'I like fast cars.'

Her frigid tone could've produced glaciers in the Pacific.

'Yours?'

'What do you think?'

She took her eyes off the road for a second, her withering glare speaking volumes.

O-kay, maybe they'd got off on the wrong foot, what with him virtually accusing her of working for Pop for easy access to his fortune. And while the car only served to reinforce his suspicions, he'd get more out of her by treating her nicely rather than antagonising further.

Not that it would be simple. He liked teasing her, getting her all riled up so those big green eyes glowed and her mouth pursed, plumping up some seriously kissable lips.

'Seeing as we're stuck with each other for the next fortnight, why don't we call a truce? I won't accuse you of anything if you stop looking at me like something you stepped in at a dog show.'

The corners of her delectable mouth twitched and as the car eased to a stop at a traffic light she shot him a tight smile.

'Can't make any promises but I'll try. Deal?'

He couldn't shake her hand, with one on the steering wheel and the other on the gear stick, so he did the next best thing. Unable to stop the resident demon that prompted him to do impulsive things on a daily basis, he leaned across and kissed her.

'Deal,' he murmured against her lips, taking advantage of her shock by kissing her again, lingering this time, sliding his lips over hers, exerting just enough pressure to show that given half a chance he'd deepen it to the point of no return.

Two sharp honks on a horn behind them had her cursing and shoving him away before she returned her hand to the gear stick and slid into first.

'Care to explain what that was about?'

Her tone had resumed its frostiness while he couldn't wipe the grin off his face.

'Not that I usually need to explain why I kiss a beautiful woman, but we couldn't shake on the deal so I did the next best thing. Why, did I offend you?'

His silky tone garnered a snort in response. 'Newsflash. That out-of-line kiss rendered the deal null and void. New deal. We don't talk for the next fortnight. Capish?'

Oh, yeah, that kiss had got to her.

'Where's the fun in that?'

'You're here to manage the finances, not have fun.'

'Surely the two aren't mutually exclusive?'

She screeched into a side street, giving him momentary whiplash, before cutting the engine and turning to face him.

'Another newsflash. I'm not one of your bimbos. I work for your grandfather. I take my job seriously. And I don't need some goof-off blow-in making trouble for me. Got it?'

She stopped just short of jabbing him in the chest. Pity, he would've liked to feel her hands on him again.

'Loud and clear.'

Her shoulders sagged in relief, before he added, 'Doesn't mean I'll play nice.'

'You're a pain in the—'

'With all this talk of work, doesn't sound like you have much time for fun?'

'I have plenty of fun.'

His snort deepened her indignant frown. 'When's the last time you had a date?'

She clamped her lips shut.

'Had sex?'

Her legs followed suit and he laughed.

'Look, we can do this the hard way or the fun way. My mouth? Has a life of its own. Runs away all the time. I'll compliment you constantly. I'll tease you incessantly. I may even kiss you on occasion but it's harmless. All good, clean fun.'

It was her turn to snort but not before he'd caught the

gleam of excitement making the gold flecks in her green eyes glow.

'No kissing.'

He paused for a moment, pretended to think. 'Sorry, can't promise that.'

'You're impossible!'

'But you like me anyway.'

Their gazes locked and the car's tight confines shrank further. He could smell her light floral perfume, could see the indecision warring with excitement in her eyes, could sense her capitulation as her shoulders relaxed and she leaned forward a fraction.

For once, he kept his big mouth shut, enjoying the electricity buzzing between them, savouring the promise of sparring, sparks and sex.

And there would be sex, he had no doubt. They had some serious chemistry going on, the kind you couldn't ignore.

Throw in the fact they'd be together twenty-four-seven and it was inevitable.

He could hardly wait.

'There's nothing I can say that'll make you back off, is there?'

'No.'

With an exasperated sigh, she shook her head. 'Having you tag along on this tour goes way beyond the call of duty. And I have to put up with grief to boot?'

She revved the engine, the sound of the firing cylinders a joy to a guy's heart.

'Go on, admit it.'

'What?'

'You're having fun already.'

With another neck-twisting wrench on the steering wheel she pulled back onto the road.

'Does it look like I'm having fun?'

'Either you're trialling for the Grand Prix or you're driving like a maniac because you're ticked off.'

She threw in another rev for good measure.

'Okay, got the message loud and clear. I'll shut up 'til we get to Ballarat.'

Her hands instantly relaxed on the steering wheel.

'How long?'

'An hour, maybe ninety minutes in this traffic,' she said, her tone smug.

He let her have her little victory for now.

She'd soon learn he didn't always do as he said.

CHAPTER THREE

CHARLI cranked up the stereo as they left the city traffic behind, hoping Luca would get the hint. She'd tried telling him to his face; it had done nothing. Maybe the subtle approach would work better?

Yeah, and maybe he'd shut up for the duration of the tour. Absolutely no chance.

Ever since he'd kissed her she'd avoided looking at him; couldn't look at him, really, not without staring at his mouth. And if she did that… She could verbally flay him all she liked but her eyes couldn't lie. One look and he'd know exactly how his kiss affected her: rattled beyond belief.

Forget the fact she hadn't had a date in nine months let alone a hint of a smooch. Abstinence couldn't explain her irrational, overwhelming urge to keep kissing him until they were breathless, the urge to run her hands all over him, the urge to tear her clothes off and straddle him and let him prove to her if half of what she'd read about his playboy reputation was true.

A car overtook them on the freeway, the four-wheel-drive's tail-lights seeming to wink at her and she blinked. Even damn inanimate objects were laughing at her expense.

How stupid could she be? The kiss meant nothing,

was more of the same teasing he'd been doing ever since she'd had the misfortune to knock on his hotel door.

For some unknown reason he'd wanted to rile her the second he'd opened the door to her wearing a towel and that infuriatingly cocky smile. So far, he'd done a good job of it. He'd flirted with her, insulted her and kissed her, all within the first hour. Didn't bode well for the rest of the fortnight.

'We nearly there yet?'

'What are you? Four?'

Slowing to let a truck pass, she smirked. 'Silly me, that's just your IQ.'

He chuckled, a low, throaty sound that rippled over her like soft velvet.

'I love it when you're feisty.'

'I love it when you're silent.'

She turned up the music, unconsciously humming along with her favourite pop ballad. Of course he had to go one better, singing along in perfect tune, the lyrics sounding like erotic pillow talk tripping from his lips.

She gulped, her hands clenching the steering wheel so tight her knuckles stood out. A hot flush started somewhere in the vicinity of her belly and spread upwards and outwards, burning her up from the inside out as he crooned about touching and pleasure and all night long.

'Interesting taste in music,' he said when the song thankfully ended and she sighed in relief.

'I like pop. Didn't peg you for a fan, though.'

'Why's that?'

'Don't guys go in for heavier stuff?'

She jumped when he reached across and squeezed her hand on the gear stick.

'Thought you'd have figured out by now, I'm not your average guy.'

'No, you're more annoying than most.'

Though that was a lie. Sure, he'd done his best to wind her up when they first met, was still doing it in fact, but he wasn't annoying so much as intriguing. And that was what made her mad; that she'd been all set to dislike him, and every time he opened his mouth only reinforced the fact, but she couldn't.

He was the first guy in ages to pique her interest, to make her want to retaliate. *The first guy to make her body tingle from top to toe, to make her skin prickle with awareness, to make her yearn for more than a teasing brush of his lips.*

'Why don't you admit it?'

Grateful she had to focus on the freeway, she didn't need to look his way to hear the laughter in his voice.

'Admit what?'

'That I'm growing on you.'

'Yeah, like fungus.'

'Now who's the child? Didn't that one get used around third grade?'

'Should be about your level, then.'

She saw him recline his seat out of the corner of her eye and wriggle around to get comfortable before clasping his hands behind his head.

'You know, I've been around the block a few times. Dated princesses, movie stars, models. But you, you're something else.'

She didn't know if he'd just complimented or insulted her but the thought of him being with all those women served as a wake-up call. He'd said it himself. He'd been around and no way was she foolish enough to become another string on his guitar.

'So you've slept around a lot. Doesn't make you a good judge of women.'

'Who said anything about sleeping around?'

She blushed, hating how she'd have to dig herself out of this one.

'You did—'

'I said dating. Not the same thing. Do you sleep with all the guys you date?'

''Course not!'

Besides, she'd have to date to have a chance at sleeping with them and she'd been so busy these past few years, proving herself, proving to Hector he hadn't made a mistake taking in a scruff like her, she'd had limited down time. When she had dated she'd chosen guys so removed from her past that once they got beyond the first few dates she found they had nothing in common.

Ironic, the cool musos who once held so much appeal left her dead now. She'd seen what that world could do, the havoc it wrought if you got caught up in the glamour and the rush, and thankfully she'd never been inclined to date Landry's clientele.

'You seeing anyone?'

'Like that'd stop you,' she muttered, shooting him a withering glance as he held up his hands in surrender.

'Hey, I like a challenge but I don't poach.'

'What's it to you anyway?'

Her heart stuttered when he leaned across, their shoulders brushing, and it took all her concentration to focus on the freeway and not land them in a ditch.

'We're both single. We're stuck together for this tour. We're attracted to each other. You do the math.'

'One plus one equals a bit fat zero?'

Disappointingly he didn't retaliate, the loaded silence only serving to notch up the intimacy, and she silently swore. This car was her pride and joy, a symbol of how hard she'd worked, how far she'd come but right now the interior she usually found comfortingly cosy seemed stifling.

It was him, of course, with his big chest and big shoulders and big head.

'Care to lay a wager on that?'

She bit back her first response of where he could stick his wager.

'Because from where I'm sitting, the two of us getting together by the end of this tour is inevitable.'

This time, her cursing wasn't so silent and she clenched the steering wheel, not risking a glance in his direction and catching the smug grin that had to be plastered across his too-handsome face.

The guy was infuriating.

The guy was annoying.

The guy was only verbalising what she'd already envisaged in her mixed-up head, making her mad as hell.

She cranked up the music and he wisely shut up. If only he'd stay mute for the rest of the tour.

The road trip from hell got worse the moment Charli approached the front desk of the apartments where they were staying.

'Welcome to Ballarat, Miss Chambers.'

'Thanks. Do you have our room keys?'

The receptionist's smile faded. 'We do but there's been a problem.'

Charli didn't need any more problems. Bad enough she had one big problem tagging along for the tour.

'What's up?'

The receptionist's eyes widened and her jaw sagged as Luca strode into the small reception area.

The woman had to be fiftysomething but she had a pulse and any woman would've drooled over Luca—including her, sadly, considering she couldn't stop thinking about that kiss the entire drive.

'I thought I told you to wait in the car,' she muttered, shooting him a frown that only served to widen his permanent grin.

Leaning down, he murmured in her ear, 'Heads-up. I'm a big boy now. I don't always do as I'm told.'

She gulped at the hint of danger tinged with promise in his smoother-than-honey tone, grateful when the receptionist held out a pair of key cards.

'Management's apologies, but due to the construction work next door and burst water mains we've had to put you both in the same apartment. It's a two-bedroom, far end of the corridor. If you need anything—'

'But I made this booking a month ago. You must have another apartment.'

Her voice had risen to an embarrassing squeak and she clamped her lips shut as the receptionist shook her head.

'I'm sorry, Miss Chambers, this is all we've got.'

Her brusque tone held a distinct undercurrent of 'take it or leave it' and, considering this had been her last resort due to some folk festival coinciding with Storm's first gig in town booking up every last room, she had no choice.

'We'll take it,' Luca said, swiping the key cards from the receptionist with a dazzling smile that had the older woman practically purring. 'Thanks.'

'You're welcome, sir.'

Charli slumped, her heart sinking as Luca draped an

arm over her shoulders and drawled, 'Let's go, roomie. I'm looking forward to bunking down.'

She elbowed him in the ribs, hard.

As Luca opened the door to their apartment and gestured her in Charli realised things could be worse. The apartment complex might've shoved them into a one-bedroom. But as she stepped into the apartment, only slightly larger than a shoebox, her relief was short-lived.

In a place this size she'd be forced to interact with Luca whether she liked it or not. Either that or spend every spare second when she wasn't working in her bedroom and, considering that consisted of a narrow bed and little else, it'd get mighty uncomfortable mighty fast.

With her blood pressure spiking along with her temper, she snatched up her overnight bag and strode into the closest bedroom, flinging it onto the bed and bumping her elbow on the door in the process.

Luca watching her in silent amusement didn't help and she stalked towards him, every step bringing her closer to slugging him. He must've caught the maniacal gleam in her eyes for he quickly shut the door and held up his hands in surrender.

'Hey, I'm not the bad guy here. You made the bookings. I'm just tagging along as your new finance manager, remember?'

'How could I forget?'

She stood toe to toe with him, wanting to hit him for no other reason than he was convenient and she had to take her temper out on someone. She wasn't the fiery type usually, had learned to master her emotions and hide them beneath a veneer of indifference, the only way to cope with her manic mother's mood swings and total disregard for her only child.

But her temper had been building the entire trip and she had to find a release before she exploded. *Temper or something else?* She banished the thought in an instant, not willing to acknowledge that this wild, out-of-control feeling had more to do with sexual tension than anger.

But it was there, simmering between them, and when she locked gazes with his the air between them shimmered and coalesced into something bigger than the both of them.

Her heart stalled when he reached for her, the crackle of electricity zapping her into reality.

She had a job to do, he had his. That was it.

She'd manage Storm, he'd manage the money. Co-workers, that was what they were for the next fortnight. That was all. And if her momentary reality flash wasn't enough, the fact he was Hector's grandson, the man she owed everything to, should be enough of a wake-up call.

Dragging in several shaky breaths, she placed a hand on his chest to stall him.

'Ignoring this isn't going to make it go away,' he said, his heat burning her through the cotton of his shirt.

'Maybe not, but I have to try.'

With a reluctant sigh, she patted his chest and walked away, his gaze burning her back until she shut the door on her stupidity and quite possibly the best offer she'd had in a long time.

Charli was going stir crazy.

She'd holed up in her room for half an hour: unpacking, unravelling, unhinged.

If she couldn't spend two nights in the same apartment

as Luca what chance did she have surviving the rest of the week? Storm had several gigs scattered through country Victoria over the next seven days, a warm-up for his big Melbourne debut in a fortnight.

She'd co-ordinated his itinerary to within an inch and then he'd thrown a spanner in the works, announcing his kid would be tagging along. From what she'd seen, rock tours were the last place for kids but in true Landry Records style she'd adjusted the itinerary to include fun kid stuff in Storm's down time.

It had all been running smoothly since that slight hiccup until Hector had fired Klaus and Luca had taken his place on tour. From what she'd learned with a few discreet inquiries, the guy could handle money. Sadly, she feared he could handle her as easily.

She paced the postage-stamp-size room, tossing around different scenarios in her head of how this could pan out.

She could avoid him other than the work stuff scheduled. She could feign politeness and spend the least amount of time with him possible. Or she could go out there and face Luca as she'd faced every other challenge in her life: with head held high, with bravado, with the confidence she could handle whatever he dished up and more.

Besides, since when had she run from a challenge? Her job presented challenges on a daily basis, from placating irate fans who couldn't get VIP tickets to ego stroking the latest chart topper and everything in between.

So what was one cocky, charming playboy? She should be able to handle him with her eyes closed. Therein lay the problem: if she closed her eyes, she could envision exactly how she'd like to handle him and it sure as hell wasn't in a professional manner.

How could she have the hots for someone she seriously wanted to strangle? He'd done nothing but goad her, tease her and throw her off balance since they'd met. And she still had no idea what he was doing here: back in Melbourne, doing Pop a favour when he'd practically ignored his existence until now?

What would a hotshot playboy want with filling in a temp job in the music industry?

Unless Pop was grooming him to take over.

Her eyes flew open as horror lodged in her gut.

No way.

Hector was at the top of his game, a fit seventy and showing no sign of slowing. Dynamic, knowledgeable, an entrepreneur with brains and morals, Hector could rule the music industry in Australia for the next decade. But once the thought had taken form it blossomed into a nasty suspicion that wouldn't go away.

Luca Petrelli as her boss? She'd rather work for her illustrious charge Storm Varth, Australia's oldest, crankiest rock star who went through personal assistants as fast as girlfriends.

She had to know why Luca was really here. Now.

Flinging her bedroom door open, she marched out into the lounge room, ready to take him on. And promptly deflated when she caught sight of the meal he'd laid out on the coffee table.

While she'd alternated between fuming and sulking in her room, he'd ducked out to the shops and bought a gourmet picnic, the staggering array of cheeses, cold meats and grilled vegetables making her mouth water.

Her stomach rumbled as the tantalising aroma of garlic-infused Turkish bread and chilli olives wafted over her and she realised how long it had been since she'd last eaten. Breakfast, eight hours ago? She'd been too wound up since then: picking up Luca, the drive here, getting a grip on her crazy behaviour—like allowing him to kiss her.

Unable to resist the lure of food she plopped onto one of the sofas just as Luca stepped out of his bedroom, and she could've sworn she salivated more at the sight of him than the antipasto platter.

He'd changed into running shorts that revealed long, muscular legs, and a white T-shirt that set off his tan, and all she could think about was how hungry she was. But not for food.

'Going for a run?'

His mouth quirked into a crooked smile that made her heart flutter wildly.

'Yeah, thought I'd leave you to eat in peace.'

She swallowed her disappointment. Probably for the best. She'd confront him better on a full stomach.

'Okay.'

He stalked towards her and she held her breath as he squatted next to her, his forearm brushing her thigh. 'Unless you want me to stay?'

She should fob him off, get rid of him so she could strategise how she'd confront him later.

Instead, she found herself nodding. 'There's an awful lot of food here, shame to let it go to waste.'

His knowing grin had her wiggling in discomfort. He knew exactly what her concession meant: she wanted him to share this meal with her for no other reason than she liked him. Liked sparring with him, liked his flirting, liked how he made her feel alive.

Letting her hair slide forward to hide her blush, she

grabbed a plate and filled it with a selection of olives, salami, Brie and Turkish bread.

'Thanks for this. It looks great.'

'You're welcome.'

Folding his frame into the chair next to her, he helped himself, slathered hummus onto bread and piled it high with semi-dried tomatoes, grilled eggplant and roasted capsicum.

'Beryl at Reception pointed me in the right direction of a local deli within walking distance.'

'Bet you smiled and she fell all over you.'

He shrugged, his modest grin endearing. 'Pity this legendary charm you attribute to me doesn't work on you.'

Oh, it was working all right. She'd only met him a few hours ago yet she felt strangely comfortable sitting here sharing an impromptu indoor picnic.

She didn't trust easily, never let anyone get too close, so the fact she'd invited Luca to join her spoke volumes.

'I'm immune,' she said, forking olives into her mouth, almost choking when he patted her knee.

'That's what they all say.'

'I bet.'

Her wry smile made him laugh and she joined in, some of her animosity towards him fading. It wasn't any secret the guy was a world-renowned playboy. Pick up a glossy magazine and Luca's picture would be in it: strutting the red carpet with an Oscar nominee on his arm, frolicking in the Caribbean ocean, driving a fast car in Monte Carlo.

He never hid who he was. Pity she couldn't say the same.

'So what are you doing here?'

'Thought that would've been obvious.'

The corners of his eyes crinkled adorably as he winked. 'Having dinner with a beautiful woman.'

She snorted. 'Why are you in Melbourne, filling in on the tour?'

When his smile faded, she pushed. 'Helping Hector when you haven't seen him in ten years?'

'That's none of your business.'

If he thought his cold, clipped tone would shut her up, he could think again.

'Actually, it is. Hector's a friend as well as my boss and I don't want anyone taking advantage of him.'

'Funny, that's what I thought about you when we first met.'

Hating that she had to justify herself to him, she toyed with the food on her plate.

'Hector's my mentor. He gave me my first break when I was a teenager looking for a job.'

And a home and a life off the streets, where she'd had to live for a horrific fortnight that haunted her for years afterwards. But Luca was on a need-to-know basis and the depth of her caring for Hector had nothing to do with him.

'I respect him more than anyone, would never take advantage of him.'

He pinned her with an intimidating glare. 'And you think I would?'

'Would you?' She shrugged, 'I wouldn't know, considering you haven't visited your grandfather in all the years I've been around.'

An emotion she couldn't fathom flickered in his eyes—regret?—before he sat back and draped an arm across the back of the sofa, his forced casualness not fooling her for a second.

'You're not going to give up, are you?'

'Nope.'

He ruffled the back of his hair, the strands curling around his fingers like caramel swirls, making her own fingers ache to delve in.

'He called me, said he was in a bind, so here I am. Satisfied?'

Not by a long shot. His trite answer hid a truth he wouldn't divulge to her: she could see it in the tense shoulders, in the rigid neck muscles, the pinch behind his smile.

There was more to him being here and if he had some nefarious plan... The food she'd just consumed roiled in her stomach. If Luca had lied to her, she'd lied to him too. Hector meant more to her than a friend and boss.

He was the man who'd taken a chance on a homeless kid when no one else had given a flying fig. He'd seen past her quick temper and resistance and resentment and opened his home, his heart and his life to her. He'd trusted her and she'd never let him down, so the thought he might not have trusted her with this...

'What's wrong?'

Luca was beside her in an instant, his concerned expression warming her heart and showing her there was more to him than lazy smiles and practised charm. She couldn't tell him the truth, that she didn't believe a word he said, so she blurted the first thing that popped into her head.

'Indigestion.'

She rubbed her chest to add authenticity and his eyes narrowed, shrewd, assessing, disbelieving.

Luca knew how to call a bluff. He'd been doing it his entire life.

'Anything I can do?'

'No, I'll be fine.'

Her bottom lip gave a convincing quiver and before he could stop himself he reached out and cupped her cheek, his thumb stroking that wobbly lip into calm.

'You sure?'

A tiny sigh puffed against his thumb; that one small vulnerability had him yearning to bundle her into his arms.

Crazy. He didn't do cuddles. He did hard and fast sex all night long; the kind of sex that didn't beg questions or require answers, the kind of sex that satisfied without complicating matters. Right now, he'd give anything to have that kind of sex with the woman staring at him with guilt in her big green eyes.

Some of what he was thinking must've shown on his face for she shuffled to her right, a subtle move to put some distance between them.

'It's not so bad. I'll live. So let's try this again. What are you doing here?'

'Already told you. Pop fired some jackass who lost the company a stack of cash and asked me to step in on this tour. Apparently Storm Varth is potentially worth a small fortune if his comeback takes off so the books need to be balanced right.'

'Why the hell would he ask you?'

His eyebrows shot up at her blunt question as she belatedly clamped her lips shut.

'I know a thing or two about companies.'

'Like how to sweet-talk receptionists and influence female CEOs?'

'Like how they run, how they can increase profit margins, how they can tighten outlays.'

Surprise widened her eyes. He liked that, catching

her off guard. She viewed him as a flake that travelled around the world, lolling on beaches doing little else.

If she only knew: being in the public eye constantly, pretending to like people who were essentially self-serving and didn't give a damn about doing anything for anybody else unless it got their greedy mugs in the glossies, dating a string of vacuous celebs to further his cause... It was damn hard work and becoming increasingly tough.

He'd done it for years now, ensuring charities were financially viable, especially those with underprivileged kids—the kind of kid he would've been if it hadn't been for Hector's generosity.

With every dollar he took from the rich who could afford it, with every dollar bestowed on those kids who needed it, he released some of his pent-up bitterness at the past. He still had a long way to go.

'You did a finance degree?'

'Economics and marketing at uni. Stuff like that interests me.'

Or more to the point, how companies could invest in his pet projects, the things that really mattered.

Her astute stare bored into him and he sat back, clasped his hands behind his head, the epitome of a guy who didn't give a damn. And he usually didn't but there was something about this woman, some indefinable quality that made him want her to like him.

'You really are an international man of mystery, aren't you?'

He winked. 'That's Petrelli, Luca Petrelli to you.'

Her mouth relaxed into a soft smile, kicking him in the guts. Or lower to be precise. That kiss in the car had been a mere prelude. Those beautiful lips, the lush full bottom lip, begged to be kissed. Repeatedly. All night long.

She stood abruptly and he mentally kicked himself for letting his thoughts drift south when they'd been getting along, establishing some kind of fragile rapport.

'Thanks for dinner. It was great.'

'My pleasure.'

Her gaze locked on his, his last word hanging in the silence between them, promising so much if she'd let herself go.

She wanted to; he could see it in the pulse beating frantically in her neck, in her slightly parted lips, in the shimmer of her eyes.

Then she blinked, straightened and the invisible thread holding them spellbound vanished in an instant.

'See you in the morning. Eight sharp.'

'Eight it is.'

She managed a tight smile at his half salute before diving for the safety of her bedroom.

Beautiful Charli could run but she couldn't hide. The spark between them was intangible but it was there and he had every intention of creating a few more before this tour was out.

CHAPTER FOUR

CHARLI stretched her neck from side to side, trying to work out the kinks. Stupid hard pillows. Though she knew the pain in her neck had more to do with her constant tossing all night while mentally rehashing conversations with Luca—and remembering him in that damn towel—than any pillow.

She didn't want to like him, didn't want to feel anything for him, but after that thoughtful dinner he'd set out last night and that *moment* they'd shared, she'd thought of little else all night but how easy it would be to succumb to his many charms.

Blowing out an exasperated huff, she knocked on Storm's door again. Her first knock had been loud enough to rouse half of Ballarat but not so much as a curtain had twitched behind the heavily tinted windows of the longest bus she'd ever seen.

She'd organised many tour buses over the years but Storm had insisted he bring his own, and after seeing the gigantic two-semi-length monstrosity painted glossy black with his signature storm clouds and lightning bolts slashing the sides, she knew why. It signalled showman.

As for the inside, she hadn't seen it, thanks to Storm living up to his superlative cranky reputation yesterday and holing away inside the bus, corresponding with her via terse text messages.

Today, she'd set the tour ground rules and make sure the idiosyncratic rocker played her way.

Her hand clenched into a fist and rapped for the third time, on the window this time, not stopping until she glimpsed a flicker of curtain.

Charli waited while Storm played his little mind games—she'd heard he was notoriously late, notoriously rude, just plain notorious—mentally checking the list she'd made on Landry Records' latest star.

Storm Varth: fifty-six, had topped world charts for eight weeks running thirty years ago, had a string of bad songs to his name over the past few decades and a string of bad women.

He'd been in rehab five times, in love ten and had finally sobered up enough over the past year for Hector to take a chance on reviving his career.

Personally, she had her doubts on the hard-living rocker lasting the distance this tour let alone making another recording but Hector had a good eye for talent, old or otherwise, so she'd make sure she did a damn good job no matter how much she wanted to throttle him.

'Take your time, Mr Varth. The longer you take with your day itinerary, the less time you'll have for trawling bars tonight.'

She bit back a grin as she heard fiddling with the lock accompanied by a string of curses before the door finally opened.

'Good morning.'

She gave him her best fake smile, designed to dazzle with just a hint of 'don't mess with me' thrown in.

'What's so freaking good about it?'

When Storm finally stepped into view, she bit the inside of her cheek to stop from laughing out loud.

Fifty-six-year-old guys shouldn't wear mid-thigh emerald silk kimonos, no matter how rich or famous.

'You've studied the itinerary for today?'

He leered at her through bleary eyes, his blond-tipped three-inch spikes standing to attention as he ruffled his hair.

'Would rather study you, sweetheart.'

She rolled her eyes. 'We've already been through this. Me, tour manager, you, rock star. Professional relationship, *comprende*?'

'I love it when you talk foreign.'

Hanging onto the door, he leaned so far forward he almost tumbled out of the bus and she couldn't help but laugh.

'Come on, Storm, play nice.'

Before he could make another innuendo about playing with her, she held up her hand.

'Get dressed. Eat. Sign the rest of those promo photos—'

'Yeah, yeah, I remember, then we tour the local music shops, sweet-talk the owners into promoting the concert tomorrow night, yada, yada, yada.'

He waved his hand around, making the kimono gape in front and she quickly averted her eyes before she got more than an unwanted glimpse of greying chest hair and fake-tan flabby abs.

'And if you're on your best behaviour, you'll get the afternoon off to visit Sovereign Hill.'

For the first time this morning his expression turned animated. 'Yeah, Tiger mentioned it looked cool on the Net.'

'Kids love it,' she said, a small part of her cynical

heart softening at his obvious affection for his seven-year-old kid. Though how anyone could name their child Tiger was beyond her. 'So snap to it.'

His lips curved into a wicked grin and for a second she could see what countless groupies over the years must've found appealing.

'I'll be much quicker if you come in here and scrub my back?'

Biting back an answering grin, she jabbed a finger in his direction.

'I'll scrub you out in a minute if you don't hop to it. Now go!'

She just caught his muttered, 'With legs like those, can't blame a guy for trying,' as he blew her a kiss and shut the door.

Shaking her head, she fished around in her handbag for her mobile, the hairs on the nape of her neck standing to attention as she sensed Luca's presence before he spoke.

'You handled him like a pro.'

'It's my job,' she said, her breath catching as she glanced up to see Luca in head-to-toe black: black silk shirt, black trousers, black shoes.

He looked like a corporate raider rather than a corporate financier and she instantly dismissed the briefest yearning for what it would be like for him to make a raid on her.

'The guy's a lech.'

'The guy probably comes on to every woman who enters his sphere every day. I can handle it.'

His blue eyes flashed with amusement as he folded his arms and propped against the side of the bus.

'So if I step out of line, will I get that professional death glare you gave him?'

'Nothing surer.'

Finally locating her phone, she scanned her calendar for the umpteenth time this morning, wanting to make sure they were on time at every scheduled stop.

'By the way, did you get the updated schedule I emailed you?'

He tapped his head. 'Got it. Memorised it.'

'Good. Because I don't want any hold-ups today. We need to get into those music stores, talk up the concert, promo the—'

'You always this hyper first thing in the morning?'

She didn't know what stalled her pulse more: his hand resting lightly on her forearm as her thumb tapped manically on her mobile keypad or the curious glint in his eyes, turning them a darker, seductive indigo.

'Always.'

Shrugging his hand off, she scrolled through the key locations for the morning, her gaze focused on the screen.

For some reason, his laid-back attitude annoyed her. This tour was a big deal and while he probably didn't give two hoots how it panned out, considering he'd be gone in a fortnight, she expected professionalism.

Liar.

Every thought since he'd opened that hotel door had been one-hundred-per-cent unprofessional.

'I know what I'm doing, if that's what you're worried about.'

Her head snapped up and she glared at him. Another thing that annoyed her: his ability to read her when she hardly knew the guy.

'You handle big money, so you said last night.' With a last glance at her phone, she shoved it back in her bag. 'How about you do your job and I'll do mine?'

His lips twitched. 'Sounds like the spiel you just gave old Lightning.'

She couldn't stop the smile tugging at her mouth. 'His name's Storm.'

'What sort of a lame-assed name is that?'

'A rock star's name, a rock star who is going to make your grandfather a lot of money if this tour goes off without a hitch so let's make sure nothing goes wrong, okay?'

He held his hands up and backed away. 'Hey, I'm just the money guy. You get to keep old Storm in line.'

'Lucky me,' she muttered, her attention captured by a curtain halfway down the bus being yanked open with Storm framed in the window doing a slow strip with his kimono while mouthing words to a song she couldn't hear, his cocky grin infuriatingly smug.

Luca registered the momentary shock on her face and turned quickly, craning his neck, only to see an empty window where the reprobate rocker had disappeared.

He frowned. 'I swear, if that old fool steps out of line with you, I'll—'

'Refer to my better judgement and skills in handling anything this job throws my way, including rockers hell-bent on clinging to their misspent youth.'

His lips compressed in an unimpressed line and a small part of her melted under his chivalry.

She didn't need protection but the fact Luca was willing to defend her honour made her like him all the more.

'Come on, let's run through the projected figures for the concert while we wait for his lordship to beautify himself.'

'With that ugly mug, it'll take him a week at least.'

She laughed and fell into step beside him. 'We can't all be like you.'

The minute the words tripped from her tongue she wished she could take them back.

'Like me?'

Floundering, she blurted, 'Well dressed. Well put together.'

Little wonder he wore a smug grin. She rolled her eyes. 'You know what I mean.'

'Thanks,' he said, touching her arm, the merest brush of his fingertips eliciting a bolt of electricity that zapped her into a heightened awareness instantly.

They had work to do.

They had a fortnight to make this the best damn tour Landry Records had ever backed.

They had a petulant rock star and his kid to please, fans to woo, crowds to draw in droves.

Yet in that moment all she could think about was how much she'd like to explore this incredibly strong attraction between them.

Gritting her teeth, she picked up the pace, resolving to focus on work.

Work was her life.

Work kept her focused and grounded and confident in a world she'd created, a world filled with certainty and guidelines, the complete opposite of her past.

No way, no how, would she let some guy, no matter how gorgeous and charming, muck up her equilibrium.

She ignored the tiny voice deep inside that whispered, *What if he already has?*

'This part of your job description?'

Charli glanced up at Luca from where she was squatting next to a river of water, a flat pan in hand.

'Whatever it takes to get the job done.'

Luca smiled as she wobbled and almost fell into the water. 'Dedication, I like that.'

'It's not you I'm trying to impress,' she said, jerking her thumb towards Storm several metres away, squatting next to his son, the two of them engrossed in sifting sand and water through the pans in search of elusive gold.

'Our resident rock star insisted I tag along on this expedition or he'd forget to set his alarm tomorrow morning.'

'The guy's a jerk,' he said, but there was no venom in his tone as he stared at Storm and Tiger, their closeness hitting him like a prize fighter's knockout punch.

For all his faults—according to the tabloids Storm had many—the guy was seriously into his son and Luca couldn't help but admire him for it.

What he would've given for a father who cared about him… The old bitterness flared, burning deep, and he absent-mindedly rubbed his chest where a permanent ache once resided.

Not any more. He'd done everything he could to eradicate his past, to come to terms with it, to ignore the mockery Rad had made of the term *father*.

Using her shovel as a prop to stand, Charli winced as she straightened her back.

'Panning for gold is killer on a girl's manicure.'

She didn't fool him for a minute. Since they'd arrived at Sovereign Hill, a recreation of a settlement from the early gold-rush days, she'd run around like a kid along-side Tiger, her enthusiasm catching.

He'd never been here; his mum had always been too busy for a day away from the city. She'd been a worka-holic, a part-time mum who'd only had him as a means to an end. Shame that her nefarious plan to entrap the

great Rad Landry never worked: the minute he'd learned
his mistress was pregnant he'd dumped her, and none of
her pitiful attempts to stay in contact could change the
fact Rad hadn't wanted a bar of either of them.

It had killed her in the end, her unrelenting, unre-
quited love for the cold bastard. He'd been numb when
Rad's light plane crashed in the Blue Mountains, killing
the father he never knew, but when his mum died a few
weeks later from what he always suspected was a broken
heart, he'd cursed and ranted at the injustice of it all,
fleeing Melbourne without a backwards glance.

'Want to give it a go?'

Charli held out her shovel to him, an unspoken question in her beautiful green eyes, and he deliberately blot-
ted out the bitterness of the past casting a blight on this
day.

'No, thanks, I'll leave it to the experts.'

Studying her blistered palm, she held it up for him to
inspect. 'Yeah, that's me, a real expert.'

Her rueful chuckle made him want to grab her palm
and kiss away those blisters.

'Admit it. You wanted to play here as much as
Tiger.'

'My secret's out.'

She smiled and it slugged him, the impact of those
glossed curving lips as startling as the underlying attraction buzzing between them.

He wasn't a fool. He adored women; loved their long
legs and lush curves and provocative eyes, their soft
laughter and look-away glances and coy smiles.

But there was something special about Charli...
Maybe the hint of vulnerability beneath the tough pro-
fessional façade, the glib no-nonsense way she handled
Storm, the way she'd looked curled up on the couch last

night, warm and relaxed in a way that appealed to him on some deeper level… Whatever it was, she intrigued him as no other woman ever had, the thought alone enough to send him bolting back to London without looking back.

But she wasn't the only professional around here: he had a job to do and the sooner they got through this tour, the sooner he could head back to the life he'd built for himself: tangle-free, emotion-free, commitment-free.

She jabbed her shovel in the dirt, leaned on it, giving a subtle jerk of her head in Storm's direction. 'When I first heard Storm was dragging along his illegitimate brat on this tour, I had visions of tantrums, but Tiger's a real sweetheart. Nothing like his dad.'

He froze, a sliver of disgust wiggling deep in a place he'd shut off years earlier. He hated that word: *illegitimate*. Had heard it bandied around far too often, had bore it as a slur, had spent years as a rebellious teenager trying to ignore the fact his father didn't want to have anything to do with him despite the efforts of his mum.

Bastard was the least of the insults he'd borne at the private boys' school Pop had funded for him to go to.

Charli's eyes widened, her expression stricken. 'I'm sorry, that was out of line. I didn't mean—'

'Forget it.'

He did, every day he did something to make himself proud to be a Petrelli.

She gnawed on her bottom lip, shifting from foot to foot, before blurting, 'Does it bother you?'

'Not being a real Landry? Being the famous Rad's bastard kid?'

Being shunned by the entire family bar Pop? Being ignored when Mum approached Rad in the street? Being booted out of his father's funeral, relegated to nothing status? Being sneered and jeered at during Father's Day at school because he didn't have one?

Quashing the old resentment bubbling dangerously to the surface, he shook his head.

'Mum was a fool, having an affair with an engaged guy then deliberately falling pregnant to trap him. Rad never would've married her. He dumped her so fast her head spun but that didn't stop her loving him or spending her life trying to get him to acknowledge her, and me.'

The sadness in her eyes slugged him more than her damn pity.

'Mum loved me in her own way but Rad was her world. I never knew if she really wanted a kid or I was just her tool as easy access to Rad's fortune but, whatever her motivation, I pretty much lost respect for her when she continued to chase him all those years for no return.'

He clamped his lips shut, wishing he hadn't said half of that, wondering what it was about this woman that made him feel as if he'd known her a lifetime.

'I had no idea—'

'Yeah, that's me, the Landrys' dirty little secret.'

And despite all he'd done over the years, how far he'd run from his past, the truth still hurt.

'Now that I've bored you enough with my rundown of happy families Landry-style, why don't you stop slacking off and get back to your itinerary?'

She hesitated, dithering over whether to push him for more or console him. To his immense relief, she pulled her shovel free and handed it to him.

'Here, Mr Hotshot Financier, pull your weight. Start digging.'

When she shot him an understanding wink, she rose

further in his estimation. Most women he knew wouldn't let a juicy story go. They'd delve and probe, eager for gossip, desperate to get the dirt and a way to wheedle their way beneath his determined aloofness.

Charli did none of that. She took the heat off him, respected his privacy, and he admired her for it.

Promising Tiger they'd find gold before he and Storm returned from their underground mine tour, he grabbed the shovel and spent the next fifteen minutes trying to concentrate on shovelling silt and water into her pan as she shook off the top layer, ducked it in more water and shook it again, and not focusing on the way her butt shimmied and her breasts swayed beneath her tight pink T-shirt.

He tried hard, he really did, but by the time she was sifting her last pan of silt, he was ready to fling her over his shoulder, jog back to their apartment and pleasure her all afternoon.

'Hey, look, I found gold!'

She jumped up and down, grinning like a kid seeing Santa for the first time, brandishing her pan as if she'd discovered the Hand of Faith.

'Show me.'

'There.'

He peered into her pan, squinting, stifling a grin when he spotted a tiny fleck no bigger than an ant.

Glancing up, he saw her triumphant smile and the excited glitter turning her eyes to moss, and bit back his first teasing response, something along the lines of 'don't give up your day job'.

'Good on you,' he said, stabbing his shovel into the sand and rolling out the kinks in his neck. 'Tiger will be rapt. What's next?'

'Storm and Tiger want to do a wagon ride and gold-pouring exhibition after the mine, so we'll check that out first and leave the most important part of the itinerary 'til last.'

Clueless, he raised an eyebrow.

'The lolly shop,' she said, patting her tummy, drawing his attention and making his libido flare.

As he dragged his gaze upwards their eyes locked and the invisible sizzle of attraction that had been there from the very start blazed to life, tugging them closer against their will, insistent, undeniable.

He expected her to look away first, to mumble some excuse about getting on with it, but she stood there, her eyes sparkling with mischief, her cheeks flushed an alluring pink.

'Know what I think?'

Her tongue flicked out to moisten her bottom lip, reaction slamming into him with the force of a kiss. 'What?'

'We should skip all that other stuff and go straight for the goodies.'

He wasn't talking about sweets and she knew it, her hungry gaze dropping to his lips, lingering there, giving him the courage to slide a hand around her waist and ease her into him until their bodies moulded.

She didn't pull away. Instead, her tiny wistful sigh wheedled its way into the most unexpected place: his heart.

Hell, no.

His heart was the least likely organ affected when he had a beautiful woman in his arms. He liked it that way, deliberately focused on everything but. Yet something about Charli had him wanting to hold her, cherish her and that was enough of a wake-up call for him to drop a quick peck on her lips and release her.

'Storm and Tiger will be back any second and I'm distracting you from your job.'

Anger sparked the gold flecks in the sea of green before she blinked, eradicating any hint of emotion, yet her disappointment was almost palpable as she pulled a notebook out of her back pocket and pretended to study it.

He showed her the same respect she'd shown him earlier, giving her time to compose herself while mentally kicking himself.

He was smarter than this. He never did emotion, never allowed himself to feel. Feeling led down a one-way road to trouble and he'd be damned if he replayed the mistakes of the past.

Whatever happened with Charli—and he had no doubt something would—he'd ensure he kept it light-hearted, ensure she knew exactly where they stood.

He had a playboy reputation to uphold, a reputation he'd fostered, a reputation he relied on to keep him exactly where he liked to be: tangle-free, emotion-free.

And he'd do whatever it took to keep it that way.

CHAPTER FIVE

CHARLI marched into the Sovereign Hill lolly shop, not caring if Luca followed.

It had taken all her will power not to slug him over the past hour. Oh, she'd been the epitome of civilised professionalism, faking enthusiasm for Storm and Tiger, who'd joined them for the carriage ride and gold pouring, concentrating on the tour guides, but inside she'd been simmering.

Trouble was she didn't know whether the bulk of her anger was directed at him or herself. She'd been so close to letting him kiss her again, had practically begged for it by letting him charm her, slide an arm around her waist, pull her close…

The memory of how he'd looked at her, a potent mix of lust and tenderness, had ripped a hole in the fabric of her self-protective mantle, the one she'd honed to a fine art since her mum had kicked her out of home at sixteen.

Hector was the only person she'd allowed to get close in all these years and even he didn't know the real her: her deepest fears, her deepest wishes.

No one got that close. Ever. Yet in the instant that Luca had locked gazes with her an hour ago, it had felt as if he were seeing into her soul.

She wasn't prone to fancifulness but in that moment a scary premonition had slithered down her spine: that this man would rip the carefully constructed world she'd built apart.

'Let me guess, you're a humbug type of girl.'

She wanted to snarl *'bah humbug'* at him. Instead, she managed a tight smile and shook her head.

'Nope, aniseed drops are my favourite.'

When she reached into her purse he stilled her hand, his touch sending fire sparking through her.

'I'll get it.'

'Let me, as a sign of my gratitude for letting me tag along all morning and answering my inane questions.'

That was another problem: far from asking inane questions he'd asked insightful, probing questions about her job and what planning an itinerary for visiting rock royalty entailed. If anything, his intelligence only made him more attractive and she silently growled at her stupidity.

With compressed lips, she muttered, 'Thanks,' and proceeded to study the extensive lollipop collection while surreptitiously watching him charm the apple-cheeked assistant behind the counter.

When he'd paid, he handed her a large bag of aniseed drops and slipped a smaller bag of something into his back pocket.

'Thanks. What did you buy?'

With a wink, he tapped the side of his nose.

'A secret emergency stash in case we run out before the end of the tour and you get grumpy on me, I've got something to sweeten you up with.'

Unable to stay mad with him too long, she chuckled. 'Good plan. You tend to bug me a lot so I'm guessing you'll need those before the fortnight is out.'

'I bug you, huh?'

He held up his hands in surrender. 'Totally unintentional. Must be my dazzling personality you're not used to.'

'Yeah, something like that,' she said, wishing there were an immunisation against tall, tanned playboys with dark blond scruffy curls and deep blue eyes. She'd be first in line for vaccination.

As she opened the bag of aniseed drops a powerful waft of liquorice drifted up and tickled her nose, catapulting her back to one of her happiest childhood memories. Her mum in a rare maternal mood, taking her to the Esplanade market at St Kilda on a sunny summer Sunday, holding her hand, stopping at every stall, admiring the paintings and woodcarvings and handmade jewellery.

The tiny bag of aniseed drops had been a rare treat from a mother so wrapped up in her selfishness she barely acknowledged her daughter existed most days. And though that special Sunday had been rare, Charli had clung to the memory for years afterwards, hoping to see another glimpse of a mum she loved unreservedly but who rarely returned that love.

When Abe had moved in, the latest in a string of her mum's loser boyfriends, she hadn't expected the status quo to change: her mum fawning over her guys and not giving two hoots about her.

But that summer Abe had moved in, the summer she'd turned sixteen, things had changed.

She'd never quite figured out why though she'd had her suspicions. Abe had been a flirt, had chatted up anything in a skirt including her and, while she'd found him creepy and done her best to avoid him, she'd seen the way her mum had started looking at her.

Her mum had been jealous, of her own daughter, and had booted her out two weeks later.

'Get out and never come back.'

Even now, ten years later, she couldn't block out the cold finality in that statement from the one person in the world she'd trusted.

She'd spent two weeks on the streets, using her limited money to survive on cheap coffee and toasted sandwiches, sleeping in a shed—Hector's shed, as it turned out—and if it hadn't been for the benevolent man mourning the death of his only son at the time, who knew how her life might've turned out?

'You okay?'

She blinked away her memories and nodded at Luca, concern creasing his brow.

'Yeah, just hungry.'

She offered him the bag of aniseed drops before popping one in her mouth. 'Let's head back so I can check the concert bookings.'

He let it go but she caught him sneaking glances her way every few minutes as they headed for the car park and when she slid behind the wheel, she swivelled to face him.

'Stop looking at me like that.'

'Like what?'

'Like you care.'

The ever-present quirk of his lips faded.

'Who says I don't?'

Unable to control the flare of anger—at her mum, at her memories, at allowing herself to be in this position of caring what Luca thought—she slammed her palms on the steering wheel.

'Give me a break. Guys like you don't do emotions.'

For a second she could've sworn hurt flickered in those too-blue eyes.

'That's harsh.'

'Is it?'

She was sick of dancing around each other, sick of the crap. They were stuck together for a fortnight and she'd be damned if she let him get under her skin and tie her up in knots with his inconsistent charms.

'Correct me if I'm wrong but didn't we have a cosy little moment back there and what did you do? Back off so fast you gave me whiplash. So you're not doing emotion? Fair comment.'

His jaw clenched before he forcibly relaxed, slumping into the passenger seat.

'Fair it may be, but who says emotion has to complicate this?'

'Complicate what?'

He shook his head, caramel curls brushing the back of his neck in finger-itching disarray.

'Now you're not being fair.'

Reaching out, he captured a strand of her hair, wound it around his finger.

'Don't do that, pretend like there's nothing going on here.'

Her heart jackknifed at the intent in his eyes, the fire of desire darkening them to indigo. 'We're two single adults forced into close proximity. Stands to reason there'd be a spark of attraction.'

She sighed as he released her hair, only to sharply inhale when his hand cupped her cheek, his thumb brushing the tender skin under her chin.

'Spark? From where I'm sitting, more like an out-of-control bushfire.'

'Lucky I'm not sitting where you are, then.'

Patting his lap, he winked. 'Well come on over, then. It's mighty comfortable where I'm sitting.'

Grateful to defuse the tension between them, she smiled.

'You don't do emotions. You do sparks. Got it.'

No way would she be foolish enough to confuse the two.

'There's something else I'd like to do.'

She didn't wait for him to elaborate.

She gunned the engine and squealed away from the kerb, wishing she could drive out the new resident demon whispering in her ear that she'd like to do him too.

Luca had never understood the expression *fly on a wall*, until now.

Virtually invisible backstage, he watched Charli whirl from one crisis to another: urging slack roadies to speed up, placating irate sound guys who weren't happy with the auditorium's acoustics, ensuring Storm's wardrobe changes were hanging in the correct order.

He had to admit he'd had no idea how much hard work she put in; and that was just to get the perpetually painful Storm on stage.

How she kept her cool under Storm's constant irrational demands he'd never know. He wanted to throttle the rock star and whisk her away from all this but he'd already made the mistake of trying to ease her load and it wouldn't happen again.

He'd offered to talk sense into Storm, she'd politely declined, giving him a stern warning to stick to what he knew best, figures, while she took care of the rest.

So far he'd played by her rules but it irked every time Storm demanded sparkling water over still, dark chocolate over milk and a hamburger with the lot just before going on stage.

To his amazement Charli didn't balk, acquiescing to the reasonable requests, denying the rest. She was a powerhouse dynamo, wielding power with a velvet glove, and he couldn't help but admire her.

Throw in the fact she had some system going where she organised free tickets for disadvantaged kids and arranged for local teenage musicians to come backstage and meet the band, and he'd become a number-one ticket holder of her fan club.

'My dad's awesome.'

Luca glanced down at Tiger, his proud gaze fixed on Storm strutting around in some weird warm-up ritual involving marching steps, swinging arms and vocal scales. He looked like a hyper toy soldier, the image accentuated by his navy leather drainpipe trousers and red velvet jacket complete with epaulettes and lightning flashes adorning the slashed sleeves.

When he didn't respond, Tiger narrowed his eyes and glared at him.

'Yeah, he's impressive all right.'

Apparently satisfied with his answer, Tiger pointed to Charli.

'Is she your girlfriend?'

Luca bit back a grin at the typical blunt interrogation technique of kids the world over. 'No.'

'Because my dad likes her, you know. I can tell.'

Ignoring the instant flare of jealousy, he folded his arms and leaned against a speaker.

'How do you know?'

Tiger rolled his eyes at his apparent ignorance. ''Cos he had a thing for my nanny but when Charli started bossing him around he forgot all about Elke.'

'You always this perceptive, kid?'

Tiger shrugged. 'I know my dad. He's pretty cool most of the time.'

Luca didn't want to know about the rest of the time. From what he'd seen, Tiger was the only person Storm didn't give crap to. In fact, when the two were together, Storm almost acted human.

Was it an act for the benefit of his adoring fans? The bad boy trying to redeem himself of past sins by playing the devoted dad? It wasn't any of his business but the way Tiger idolised his dad, he'd hate for the kid to be let down.

As he'd been.

The first time he'd met his father was imprinted indelibly on his memory: he'd been five years old and his mum had taken him to see a movie at the Jam Factory on Chapel Street. He'd been beyond excited, looking forward to a treat of popcorn, fizzy soda, lolly bag and an afternoon uninterrupted with his mum, when they'd run into Rad exiting some exclusive clothing boutique.

His mum had lit up, clutching his hand tighter as they all but ran across the road to confront him. He'd been wary of the man who glared at him as if he were about to pickpocket his wallet, but he'd remembered his manners and held out his hand when his mum had introduced them.

Rad had taken one look at his outstretched hand and walked away without looking back.

His mum had pretended like it didn't matter, but he'd seen the tears in her eyes and his outing had been spoiled. He'd never been able to stomach popcorn since.

That was the first time Rad had rejected him but not the last and thankfully he'd grown a thicker skin as he'd got older. Yet glancing at Tiger, his obvious adoration for a father who was flaky at best, brought it all back in a rush—the expectations, the hope, the naivety— and he wished he could protect the kid from potential heartache.

Tiger elbowed him. 'Watch this.'

As the crowd worked into a frenzy, their stomping and clapping threatening to raise the roof, Storm paused at the main curtain, turned towards his son and gave Tiger a salute, then held up an index finger.

Tiger responded with a thumbs-up sign of approval and only then did Storm allow Charli to do one final check of his costume and wireless mike before giving him a gentle shove out onto stage.

As Storm slid across the stage to an electric-guitar riff and the crowd went wild Luca nudged Tiger.

'What were those signals about?'

Tiger grinned, his little chest puffing out. 'My dad always says I'm his number-one man, so he holds one finger up before he goes on stage. No matter if I'm back-stage or at home in bed, he'll always make the sign so I know he's thinking of me. Cool, huh?'

'Yeah, cool,' Luca said, relief filtering through him.

Despite Storm's lousy work ethic, it looked as if he loved his son, and Luca couldn't help but admire him for that.

'What you said before?'

Confused, Luca stared at Tiger. 'About?'

'About Charli not being your girlfriend? I didn't be-lieve you.'

Tiger's cheeky grin and quick glance over his shoul-der alerted him to one incoming dynamo. 'Here comes your girlfriend now.'

With a wave Tiger vanished, leaving him to handle a bright-eyed glowing Charli.

'Isn't this the best?'

She did an odd little twirl, clapping her hands like an excited kid, and he couldn't help but laugh.

'You really thrive on this stuff, don't you?'

'Uh-huh.'

She didn't need the shimmery gold eyeshadow highlighting her eyes. They gleamed and glittered all on their own, testament to how the backstage buzz turned her on.

Oh-oh, bad choice of words, silent or otherwise, and he covered his mental gaff with gruffness.

'Don't you get tired of the fawning?'

He gestured around them. 'The roadies, the band, the hangers-on. All they do is bow down to Storm no matter how much of a pain in the ass he is.'

Her smile waned and he hated himself for putting a dampener on this evening, but somewhere between Tiger's open adulation of his father and watching Charli flit around like a social butterfly he'd realised he didn't like this scene at all.

He lived it almost every day of his life—the fake platitudes, the schmoozing, the handshakes, the air kisses—and he was over it.

In all honesty, he'd grown tired of his carefully honed life a long time ago and seeing Charli in her element here disappointed him in some way.

He wanted her to be deeper than all this fluff, wanted her to care about more than whether Storm bloody Varth had his sparkling water on hand.

Harsh? Unfair? Maybe, considering she was only doing her job, but he couldn't shake the feeling the woman he'd divulged more to than he would've liked wasn't who he thought she was.

'The band and roadies listen to Storm because if it wasn't for him they wouldn't have the opportunity to have another crack at the big time.'

Where her eyes had glittered with enthusiasm a moment ago, they now radiated enough fire to scorch him on the spot.

'Are you questioning my pandering to Storm too? Because it's my job and you have no right—'

'Sorry, guess I'm not a good backstage groupie. I've got some more numbers to crunch with the booking centre so I'll see you back at the apartment.'

He squeezed her upper arm, a brief apologetic gesture that only served to reinforce how stupid he was. He wanted this woman in a way he hadn't wanted another in a long time, if ever, and alienating her by attacking her job wasn't the way to go.

'Yeah, whatever,' she said, and she was gone, her other arm claimed by some teenager with too-long hair and too many eyebrow rings, tugging her towards the stage door where some local big-shot was trying to muscle his way in.

When she flashed the pushy guy a dazzling smile, he quelled another surge of disappointment and headed for the booking office.

Charli had been the go-to person on several tours but none had had the vibe of this one.

Even now, as she watched Storm charm everyone in the tiny wine bar she'd chosen for his after-party, she couldn't shake the feeling Landry Records was on the verge of something big in backing his comeback.

An image of Luca's disapproving expression shimmered into her conscience… Well, not everyone was thrilled about it. He'd surprised her backstage. One minute he'd looked as if he was getting into the spirit, the next he'd virtually accused her of pandering to Storm because she liked it.

As the man in question snorted tequila through his nose, she maintained her unflappable stage face, the one she'd honed over the years to deal with whatever this job threw her way.

She loved this job, loved the unpredictability of it, the challenges, the moments when everything came together and the show went off without a hitch.

Like earlier, when Storm had strutted his way across the stage, belting out a medley of old hits and wooing the crowd with new stuff. He'd worked them into a frenzy, milking every last ounce of screaming adulation and applause out of them, and when he'd staggered backstage, sweat dripping in gross rivulets down his leather pants, she'd almost forgiven him for being such a pain in the butt.

If he continued to woo crowds on the country leg of this tour, the scheduled Melbourne show next week would be a sell-out. From there, fan hysteria would build for a new CD, the one Hector was trying to sign him to, and Landry Records would score a major coup in getting the legendary Storm Varth back on track, back into the studio and back on top.

Flush with optimism, she sipped her Snowball, savouring the smooth Advocaat mixed with the lemonade fizz, her usual celebratory drink.

As an angry shout came from the direction of Storm's table the drink stuck in her throat and she coughed, her heart sinking as she took in the tense scene: Storm with his hand on a pretty young thing's breast while he signed the other she offered, and a biker dude, obviously the girl's boyfriend, clenching his hands into fists.

So much for a celebration drink. With a resigned sigh she pushed her Snowball aside, pasted her best negotiator's face on and joined the fray.

In a slick move more suited to a magician she palmed an A4-size photo of Storm from her carry-all, swiped Storm's hand away from the girl's breast and deftly guided it to the photo, smiling all the while.

'I'm sorry, miss, Storm doesn't do personal autographs any more but I'm sure you'd love to have a signed picture?'

While her boyfriend blew cartoon steam out of his ears, the girl simpered and tugged up her top. 'Sure, that'd be great. Thanks, Stormie.'

When the girl made a move to kiss the rock star Charli stepped between them, shooting Storm a warning glare as she yanked the newly signed photo out of his grasp and shoved it at the girl.

'Here you go. Have a nice night.'

Groupie Girl stared at *Stormie*'s photo with open longing before sliding her hand into Biker Dude's and tugging fiercely. 'Come on, let's go see if that all-night photo store has any frames.'

With a final death glare in Storm's direction Biker Dude followed his girlfriend and Charli waited 'til they left the bar before exhaling in relief.

Shooing away the groupie on Storm's left, she sat, immediately regretting her decision when she sank into the low sofa, too close to the increasingly intoxicated star of the show.

Keeping her voice low, she hissed, 'No more signing of body parts.'

'Jealous?'

Wrinkling her nose, she waved away the toxic alcohol cloud emanating from Storm's mouth.

'Merely wanting to keep you in one piece so you have a real shot at getting the comeback you deserve.'

The petulant tightness around his mouth eased. Damn, she was good at her job.

'Where's your minder?'

He leered at her, his bloodshot eyes clear indication he'd been doing double-shot vodkas rather than the singles she'd stipulated as part of the celebration.

Annoyed—at his lack of responsibility and her missing the double shots—she glared at him.

'If you're referring to Luca he's burning the midnight oil, crunching numbers to keep your sorry ass on stage.'

When he smirked and opened his mouth to respond she made a zipping motion.

'So if I was you I'd be nice to Luca because if he pulls the plug on your funding for this tour, you can kiss your comeback goodbye.'

For the first time since they'd met she saw genuine fear in those bleary eyes. Good. Fear meant he cared and if he cared he wouldn't do anything monumentally stupid to screw this tour up. She hoped.

Turning to the group, she tapped her watch. 'Listen up, people. Great show tonight but we have to do it all again in Bendigo so last drinks.'

She held up her hands at the groans and odd expletive. 'Five more minutes then the bus leaves without you. And, considering it's minus two out there, I'd get a hurry on if I were you.'

The lead guitarist nodded and jerked a head in Storm's direction, indicating he'd make sure their star made the bus. Thank goodness one of the band members had a level head. The rest were still high on the night's success and determined to celebrate to the crack of dawn.

And as she glanced around at the motley crew of drunken guys and their hangers-on, it hit her, what Luca had seen earlier on.

She'd been abuzz with the thrill of working backstage, co-ordinating everything to the nth degree, all part of her job, but why did she really do it? Why did she really put up with crap like this?

She tried so hard to be the best, to stay in control at all times but as she looked at Storm, the epitome of the bad-boy rock stars she managed on a regular basis, it struck her that her determined drive to stay in control stemmed from more than job satisfaction.

She was afraid. Afraid of not doing a good job and getting sacked, afraid of being judged not good enough, afraid of feeling helpless and worthless and rejected, the same way she'd felt when her own mother didn't want her.

Doing a great job every day obliterated that fear: the harder she worked, the better she performed, the easier to forget that her job *was* her life. She loved it. She thrived on it. That wasn't so bad, was it?

Yet something in Luca's disappointment, as if he viewed her world as shallow, grated. And that was what scared her the most: that she valued his opinion. For a guy she'd only known a few days, what he thought mattered and it shouldn't.

She'd learned the hard way never to depend on anyone for happiness. Better to forge her own way in the world; without the approval of charming rogues with hypnotic blue eyes.

The Snowball she'd drunk earlier rolled in her belly

and she headed for the door, needing fresh air, needing fresh perspective.

She was probably overtired, that was where all these maudlin thoughts were coming from, but the more she tried to ignore the realisation that she was afraid, the more it taunted her until she deliberately blocked it out by marching back into the wine bar, settling the tab and doing a final round-up of the gang, shepherding them out to the bus.

When the last staggering band member was on board, she swung up into the front seat and gave the driver the go-ahead.

Some night. The concert had been a huge success, she'd averted potential disaster with Storm and that groupie, and no one had got into trouble.

Yet as Storm and his back-up vocalists broke out into an a cappella version of his first hit she couldn't help but wonder if she was hanging on too tight and what might happen if she loosened up a bit.

With Luca around for the next few weeks, maybe now wasn't the best time to find out.

CHAPTER SIX

HUNGER clawed at her stomach, a constant pinch that didn't ease despite her daily cup of coffee and grilled-cheese-sandwich ration.

She rubbed it, annoyed when her ragged nails scratched the dirty skin of her belly. Sneaking a wash at garden taps wasn't a patch on a nice hot shower.

When she opened her eyes, she wished she hadn't. The grimy garden shed stank of manure and had gigantic cobwebs draping the windows like lace curtains.

Something scuttled over her hand in the darkness and she bit back a scream, bolting for the door, flinging it open to see her mum.

Her mum had lost the frown that perpetually creased her forehead. She stood there, her arms wide, the most beautiful smile on her face.

'Welcome back, Charlotte.'

She ran as fast as she could, running so hard her lungs ached but the closer she got, the further away her mum seemed.

When her legs cramped and threatened to collapse out from under her, she put on one last extra burst of speed, flinging herself into her mum's arms, desperate for a hug.

She needed that hug more than anything in the world,

*needed to hear her mum say she'd made a giant mistake
and that she loved her and wanted her back.*

*Yet when she reached out, her fingers grasping, her
mum vanished and she fell headfirst down a huge dark
hole…*

Charli screamed and sat bolt upright in bed, her arms
flailing, her legs tangled in the sheets.

The claustrophobic darkness pressed in on her and
she gasped for breath, dragging in big lungfuls to ease
the tightness in her chest.

As her pounding heart eased to a sedate canter rather
than an out-of-control gallop she hugged her knees to
her chest and rested her head on them.

It had been a stupid dream, a familiar one that still
haunted her on occasion.

Must've been the aniseed drops though she'd be
damned if she gave up her favourite boiled sweets. Or
maybe it had been the fear she'd let creep into her sub-
conscious at the bar earlier, undermining everything
she'd worked so hard to build up: confidence, happiness,
a career.

Damn it, she was good at what she did and no way
would she let memories of her mum ruin everything.

The bedroom door flung open and her head snapped
up, Luca's semi-naked silhouette in the doorway jump-
starting her heart all over again.

'You okay?'

'Yeah, just a nightmare.'

'Must've been a doozy.'

He hesitated in the doorway, half turned to leave, his
movement allowing the hallway light to flood her room,
and his eyes widened.

'My God, you're drenched.'

He crossed to her bed in two strides, swiping the perspiration off her brow with gentle fingers.

'Wait here, I'll get you a towel and fresh sheets.'

Her refusal died on her lips as she glimpsed the genuine concern on his face and she nodded, clamping her lips shut on a sudden sob.

She let him bring a towel and drape it around her shoulders while he changed the bed and she blinked back tears at the sight of the strong, virile playboy doing such a mundane domestic chore.

'Here.'

He held up the top sheet for her to slide under and as she sank into bed her back brushed his chest.

That was when it hit her, how truly shaken she must be from the dream, for she'd been so busy trying not to cry she hadn't registered Luca wore a pair of black silk boxers and nothing else.

He tucked her in and when he straightened to go she grabbed at his hand.

'Thanks.'

'You're welcome.'

His concern hadn't eased. If anything, he kept staring at her as if she'd fall apart at any moment.

When he tried to slide his hand out from hers, she held on tighter, suddenly desperate for him not to leave her alone. She didn't want to fall asleep, didn't want to risk another nightmare tonight.

'Stay for a minute?'

He stiffened before nodding and sinking onto the mattress, still holding her hand.

'Want to talk about it?'

She shook her head. The last thing she wanted to do was divulge the truth about her past and how screwed up she'd been as a kid.

'Not really.'

She plucked at the sheet with her free hand, sensing his reluctance to stay, wanting to keep him with her for the purely selfish reason of not being alone in the dark.

'Did you ever have stuff happen to you as a kid, stuff you wish you could change?'

He'd shifted slightly so she couldn't see his expression in the shadows but the tension in his shoulders spoke volumes.

'Yeah, doesn't everyone?'

'I never knew my dad.'

Something she'd often wondered about…was that the reason her mum hated her so much, that her dad had done a runner before she'd been born?

'Join the club,' he muttered, his bitterness audible.

Distracted from her version of non-happy families, she said, 'You mentioned not knowing your dad, so how close are you to Hector?'

He remained silent and she was racking her brain for something to break the awkward silence when he finally spoke.

'Rad didn't want a bar of me so I guess Hector tried to even out the family score. He paid for my education, set up a huge family trust I came into when I turned twenty-one, tried to maintain contact since I was a kid.'

'But?'

He shrugged, a flicker of pain slashing his features. 'But I never understood why he wanted to know me and Rad didn't.'

'Is that why you've stayed away all these years?'

She paused, gnawed on her bottom lip, knowing this was none of her business but needing to ease some of the tension radiating off him. 'Hector cares about you. He wouldn't have turned to you for help now otherwise.'

He stiffened and she mentally kicked herself for probing into his past when it obviously hurt, half expecting him to throw out a defiant, *Isn't it enough I'm here?* Instead, he turned the focus back on her.

'Was that the nightmare? Family stuff?'

She bought his distraction, not wanting to delve further when he'd obviously clammed up.

'Yeah, something like that.'

'In my experience, you can't rely on anyone but yourself. Stick to that motto and you'll be fine.'

'Isn't that too cynical?'

'Realistic,' he said, his expression shuttered as he turned and hallway light illuminated his features. 'Anyway, better let you get back to sleep.'

'Yeah, I guess.'

Neither of them moved, but her fear of being alone and letting the nightmare crowd her again made her grip his hand tighter and do something out of character.

'Stay. Please.'

His head snapped up, his gaze locking on hers.

'I'm not a saint, Charli.'

'I'm not asking you to be,' she whispered, her free hand snaking around his neck and pulling his head towards her.

She wanted to erase the darkness of her nightmare, wanted to reaffirm she was a different person from the desperate, affection-starved teenager her mum had booted out without a qualm.

Surging up from the bed, she met him halfway, their mouths clashing in an explosion of heat and passion.

That kiss in the car? A prelude to the main event, their lips eagerly seeking pleasure, hungry for more.

She clung to him, mindless to everything but him and the exquisite torture of having his tongue touch hers, tease hers, giving her a tempting taste of what it could do elsewhere.

She moaned into his mouth as his hands delved into her hair, his fingertips tugging at the roots, the momentary pain bordering on pleasure.

'Jeez,' she whispered on a sigh as he tore his mouth from hers and trailed kisses down her neck, nipping at the delicate skin with his teeth, raising goose bumps all over her body.

Her head fell back and she caught sight of them in the wardrobe mirror: their bodies melded as if one, his bronzed arms engulfing her, her skin flushed and eyes wide.

The image was wild and wanton, two people living in the moment and not caring about tomorrow.

That was when it hit her.

She was behaving just like her mother.

Sharon had continually tried to seek solace with men, desperate to obliterate the misery of her life: dead-end checkout job, living in a housing-commission flat with no money and a daughter she didn't want.

And while she was nothing like the selfish Sharon, even the slightest resemblance was enough to put a dampener on this amazing encounter.

Her hesitation cost dearly for Luca's lips eased off her neck and he held her at arm's length, studying her face.

'I knew I shouldn't have done that.'

'Don't go getting a conscience on me now,' she said, trying to lighten the moment, not wanting him to feel bad when she'd wanted this as much as him. 'Besides, I instigated this.'

'Because you needed comforting.'

He pronounced it as if he'd rather be panning for gold all night in that freezing river than be here.

She opened her mouth to deny it before clamping her lips shut.

Damn him, he was right. She'd turned to him to vanquish her deep-seated insecurities and in doing so had ended up more like her mother than she wanted to be.

'I've made a mess of this, haven't I?'

A devilish smile quirked his lips and eased her fears she'd messed up big-time.

'You needed a goodnight kiss. I gave you one. How about we leave it there for tonight?'

She nodded and brushed her fingers across his cheek in thanks, the prickle of his stubble sending a tingle from the pads of her fingers all the way up her arm.

'Okay, then.'

He stood and the bed immediately felt empty, her heart giving an alarming twinge as she watched him walk away.

He was so beautiful, the muscles in his back fluidly shifting with every step, every arm swing, as she briefly wondered how many women had watched him do the same thing.

Walk away leaving them wanting more.

He paused in the doorway, cast a crooked smile over his shoulder.

'Just for the record, the next time we do this, there'll be no comforting involved.'

Her heart ka-thumped and her body zinged in anticipation but thankfully he didn't wait for a response.

When he'd left, leaving her door open, she fell back into bed and flung her forearm over her eyes. It didn't work in blocking out his image as he'd stared at her a moment ago, a potent blend of determination, desire and drop-dead gorgeous.

He was right.

There would be a next time.

And it would blow both their minds.

CHAPTER SEVEN

HECTOR never called when she was on the road. He trusted her judgement, whether scoping out a Gold Coast theme park for a record launch or checking the Opera House for seating capacity. So when her phone buzzed with Hector's ringtone, she experienced a fleeting moment of panic.

Crazy, that even after all these years and the countless ways he'd shown her she mattered, she still expected to have all her good fortune ripped away in an instant by the man who'd bestowed it in the first place.

She should know better by now. From the moment he'd found her squatting in his shed Hector had never been anything but gallant and caring and trusting. A saviour in every sense of the word: giving her a place to live, a part-time education including gaining her high-school certificate and, later, a job in his company.

She'd made something of herself thanks to Hector. She owed it all to him so why was she edgy now?

'You answering that?'

Luca glanced up from the newspaper—the business section, not sports—and there went another preconception.

She poked her tongue out at him, grabbed the

phone and edged out onto the tiny balcony of their new accommodation.

She hadn't believed it when their booking in Bendigo had also experienced some catastrophic natural disaster—namely a ruptured sewer line—and she'd been forced to apartment share with Luca. Again.

She didn't believe in fate or anything remotely like it but if she didn't know any better Cupid, or whatever contrary god had bows and arrows, was having a belly laugh at her expense.

Taking a deep breath to quell the niggle of anxiety in her gut, she pressed the answer button on her phone.

'Hi, Hector, how are you?'

'Fine. How's the tour coming along?'

His booming voice sounded the same as usual and she exhaled in relief.

'Great. The concert in Ballarat was a sell-out and Storm's behaving...' she omitted the part where she had to drag Storm out of the wine bar before he assaulted a groupie and her guy '...and I've checked out the local attractions in Bendigo for Tiger, plus we're all set for the concert here tomorrow tonight.'

'By your use of *we*, I take it things are going well with Luca?'

The hint of concern beneath Hector's usual joviality surprised her. What did he expect, for her to boot his grandson off the tour?

'He's tolerable.'

Luca rattled his newspaper and Hector guffawed.

'You're a true professional, Charli. There'll be a bonus in this for you if you manage not to kill him by the end of the tour.'

'How much not to kill him by Sunday?'

Her sickly sweet smile raised Luca's eyebrows as

he folded the newspaper shut and beckoned for the phone.

Hector chuckled. 'We'll work something out when you get back. Any chance I can speak to him?'

'He's all yours.'

She handed the phone over to Luca and fiddled with her notebook, trying not to eavesdrop on their conversation. Not that she could divulge much from Luca's *uh-huhs*.

Curious, she dropped onto the sofa and watched him, fascinated by his interaction with Hector.

Their conversation seemed stilted, awkward, and for a guy so at ease teasing her none of his usual warmth and wit came through when talking to his grandfather.

In fact, he sounded like the employees who tiptoed around Hector, treating him like the mogul of the Aussie music scene he was, distantly polite, slightly wooden for fear of saying the wrong thing.

Luca's stiff, artificial conversation with Hector went a long way to explaining why she'd never met him before. They weren't close, which begged the question: why come to Hector's aid now?

He hung up and handed the phone back to her.

'He threatened to take away my allowance if I didn't take good care of you.'

'You get an allowance?'

'Nah, but that's what it felt like. Like I was a kid and he was telling me to do it or else.'

'I can take care of myself.'

An image of her clinging to him last night flashed into her mind, how safe he'd made her feel, making a mockery of her declaration.

He was thinking the same thing, she could see it in

the flare of understanding in his eyes but, wisely, he didn't bring it up.

'Hector's pleased with your work?'

Caution crept into his eyes, shadowing them.

'Yeah, no worries on that front.'

'How come I've never met you before?' she blurted, instantly regretting her outburst when he frowned and folded his arms.

Classic back-off posture but it was too late, her curiosity had prompted her to run off at the mouth.

'Melbourne never held much appeal even when I lived here.'

'Oh,' she muttered, suitably chastised but still not convinced.

Ten years was a hell of a long time for someone to stay away from their home city. Not that she couldn't empathise. Considering her past, she could've quite happily fled Melbourne and not looked back if it weren't for Hector rescuing her.

His frown cleared as he stepped towards her and ran a fingertip down her bare arm.

'Why? You regretting the fact we haven't met before now?'

Ducking down, he murmured in her ear, 'I know I am.'

Her forced laugh sounded brittle as she shoved him away, needing distance to prevent herself from falling into his arms the way she had last night.

'Save it. I've got work to do.'

He didn't budge. 'How much longer?'

'Another two hours at least.'

'Fine. Then we're going on a date.'

Her heart leaped for joy while her inner independent chick bristled at his commanding order.

'Maybe if you asked nicely you might have more than a snowball's chance in hell of me agreeing to a date with you.'

'Oh, you'll agree.'

To prove it, his lips brushed the tender skin behind her ear, a barely there butterfly kiss that sent a shudder of longing through her.

'You play dirty,' she muttered, all signs of resistance fleeing in the face of his heavy-duty flirting.

This time, he kissed her just shy of her mouth, his lips lingering as he murmured, 'You have no idea how dirty I can play but I'm hoping you'll soon find out.'

On a heartfelt sigh, she whirled away and headed off to finish up work for the day.

Her body throbbed with expectation, his low chuckles strumming her nerves.

Hold him at bay?

Not a hope in hell.

Luca had mucked up. He needed to establish some distance from Charli. Not in the physical sense. Oh, no, physically, he'd like to get up close and personal, the sooner the better. Emotionally? She had him ready to bolt and not look back.

Last night had been bad enough, making him feel sorry for her, making him feel helpless against her inner demons, making him feel period. Then today, after chatting with Hector, she'd stared at him with those all-seeing green eyes, probing for answers he had no intention of giving, and he'd blurted the first thing that popped into his head.

He'd asked her on a date.

He'd been so disarmed by her ability to get under his skin he hadn't been thinking straight and the instant the offer had tripped from his lips he'd wanted to take it back.

But he'd seen the spark of interest in her expressive eyes, the glitter of excitement, and he'd been stuck. Taking her on a date was not a way to maintain emotional distance so he'd focused on what he did best: flirt, woo, keep things casual.

So far, it had worked like a charm. With Storm and his entourage taking the afternoon off after an intense rehearsal this morning, they'd toured the local art galleries, strolled through the historic district, walked around Lake Weeroona and were now ensconced in the Hotel Shamrock.

'This is a grand old pub,' she said, her eyes sparkling with pleasure as she glanced around at the rich wood panelling, the gleaming brass fittings, the polished oak furniture.

Sure, the place was nice but he'd much rather stare at the beautiful woman sitting opposite, a faint flush making her cheeks glow, her eyes sparkling like emeralds.

Her tight-fitting pink jumper accentuated her curves and his hands itched to roam all over her, to complete what they'd started last night. For while his misplaced gallantry had kicked in and prevented him from taking it all the way as he craved, he hadn't forgotten how she'd felt. Soft, warm and incredibly lush.

He shifted in his chair and refocused when she raised an eyebrow in his direction.

'Some date. You aren't even listening to me.'

'I'm listening.

His hand snaked across the table and snagged hers. 'Yeah, the pub is impressive but I'd rather watch you.'

Her glossed lips softened into a smile that lit her face.

'Do those lines usually work for you?'

'You tell me.'

She laughed and he lifted her hand to his mouth, placing a kiss on her palm and wrapping her fingers around it. A little shiver rippled through her and her lips parted on a surprised O.

He loved that about her, how responsive she was. That kiss last night… He couldn't stop thinking about it, how she'd come alive in his arms, the sexy sounds she'd made.

They'd have a repeat, he had no doubt but next time they'd be taking it all the way.

She eased her hand out of his, a coy smile curving her lips.

'By that look in your eye, you're expecting this to be a full-service date.'

'I'm not expecting anything.'

And he wasn't. He wanted this date to be fun, to distract him from how much he was growing to like being with her. As for sex… Yeah, he wanted her but there was no ulterior motive.

She continued studying him with a shrewd stare. 'I'm good at reading people and from where I'm sitting you look like a guy with one thing on his mind.'

Damn, she was good.

'Two things, actually. And here comes one of them right now,' he said.

A waiter brought their steak dinners at that moment, took one look at their ga-ga expressions and scuttled away.

Smiling, she picked up her cutlery. 'What's the other thing?'

Enjoying her sassy side, he lowered his voice to just above a whisper.

'Dessert.'

She blushed and stabbed her fork in his direction. 'You're good.'

He opened his mouth to respond but she butted in, 'But I'm better. And while this date has been fabulous and I think you're charming and we share a spark, I can't help but feel you're doing this to distract me.'

Impressed by her intuition, he pushed his plate away, sat back and folded his arms.

'From?'

'Getting to the bottom of why you're really here.'

She stabbed a honeyed carrot, popped it in her mouth and chewed, giving him time to process what she'd said.

How did she do that, see right through him? Though he should be thankful; at least she hadn't cottoned onto the real motivation behind this date, creating emotional distance, ensuring she didn't get too close.

'You really think I've got some ulterior motive?'

She pinned him with a stare that would make a lesser man quiver in his boots.

'Have you?'

He didn't like the fact she doubted his motives for helping Pop, didn't like it at all, for somewhere during the past few days he'd grown to value her opinion. It mattered to him what she thought and it shouldn't, damn it.

Fostering his footloose, fancy-free image took work and it suited him just fine. Being back in Melbourne should've been a mere blip on his life plan. Yet somehow the blip had turned into a massive blooper, courtesy of the gorgeous woman staring at him with suspicion in her moss eyes.

'What do you want me to say? That I'm here to make a play for Pop's fortune? Because if that's what you think…'

He bit back the rest, the old resentment splintering the immunity he'd built against the injustice of people who thought exactly that.

It was one of the reasons he'd run all those years ago, had hated the sly looks and pointed innuendos. He'd thought he was immune to it now, had built up a hard shell the past ten years, yet having Charli imply the same disgusting motivation for him being back in Pop's life stung. More than it should. And that was what scared the crap out of him. That it was too late to establish emotional distance from her, that he already cared too much what she thought of him.

'Luca, look at me.'

He dragged his reluctant gaze from his plate, defiantly met hers.

'Sorry, I was way out of line pushing you like that. Guess I've worked for Hector a long time, I'm overprotective and I don't want him getting hurt.'

'Something you think I'd do.'

He spat the words out, hated when she flinched.

'No.'

She reached across the table, placed her small, elegant hand on his.

'Questioning your relationship with Hector is none of my business. You're here as a stand-in finance guy on this tour, the rest is your business.'

She squeezed his hand and slid hers back across the table. 'Now that I've completely botched this date, why don't we eat these fabulous meals and try and salvage something from the evening?'

'Sounds good to me.'

But as they ate their steak and made polite small-talk, he knew the rest of his plans for the evening had just gone up in a cloud of mistrust, secrets and regret.

On a scale of one to ten absolute shocker dates, Charli had no idea how to rate her date with Luca.

After the constant go, go, go of the tour, it was lovely to have an afternoon off to do the touristy stuff. And dinner at the beautiful old Hotel Shamrock had been going so well until she'd botched it.

What on earth had possessed her to push him for answers about his presence here? Why couldn't she just accept he was doing Hector a favour and be done with it?

Once she'd brought up his past and his relationship with Hector he'd clammed up. Where there'd been flirting and laughter before, after her interrogation there'd been excessive politeness and stilted small-talk.

She'd been embarrassed by her nightmare last night, by how freaked out she'd been, and in some warped mistaken idea had thought chatting about Hector and how much she cared for him might allay his fears she wasn't a complete nutter.

Lame, but what could she do? Explain that his compassion and comforting when she'd needed it most had seriously disconcerted her? That she'd felt safe in his arms in a way she hadn't in a long time?

Hector was the only person she remotely trusted these days and to think Luca had crept under her guard so easily was seriously disturbing.

She needed some space, had been hugely relieved

when they'd made it back to the apartments only to find Storm and the band hanging out in the bar next door. On the pretext of checking up on their protégé she'd hoped to end the evening, making it back to their apartment after Luca was in bed.

Yet again he'd surprised her, suggesting they have a nightcap, and she couldn't very well refuse considering she'd already said she was heading into the bar to suss out how Storm was doing.

'Here you go.'

He handed her a lemon soda and slid into the circular booth next to her, too close for comfort, too close to ignore the buzz between them.

'Thanks.'

She raised her glass, clinking against his beer. 'To a brilliant tour Storm Varth fans will never forget.'

'To a tour I'll survive without strangling Storm Varth.'

She chuckled at his tortured expression as he jerked his head in the singer's direction.

'Though he seems to be behaving himself tonight.'

If he only knew. She hadn't told him about the wine-bar incident, not deeming it relevant to his job but in reality wanting to keep the two apart.

Sure, Storm was an over-the-hill miva—her term for male divas—but he was part of her job. Luca, on the other hand, had low tolerance for their resident miva and, considering he was out of here at the end of the tour, she wouldn't put it past him to threaten to settle scores after the tour.

'He's still got it for his age.'

Luca snorted. 'Got what? Bad hair and too-tight pants?'

She smiled at his accurate description. 'Showbiz pizazz.'

They watched Storm being tugged onto a makeshift stage by the bar's owner, his fake reluctance instantly disappearing the second a microphone was thrust into his hand.

'Look at him. He's a natural.'

She ignored Luca's muttered, 'A natural jerk.'

'Must be hard to maintain a public persona for thirty-odd years. I'd hate it.'

A tiny frown creased Luca's brow as he studied her. 'I thought you loved all this hype?'

'I love the challenges of the job, the uniqueness guaranteed on a daily basis.'

She waved towards the stage where the band members had joined Storm. 'But no way could I be like those guys, feeling like I have to constantly perform. It'd drive me mad.'

His frown disappeared as he sat back against the cushions and she had the distinct feeling she'd said the right thing without meaning to.

'You're one smart woman.'

He raised his beer in her direction before taking a long slug, leaving her to ponder this complex man.

'Performing gets tiring after a while.'

He spoke so softly she wondered if she'd heard right but before she could question him further Storm and the band let rip with a golden oldie that raised the roof, leaving her to ponder Luca's revelation while the few patrons dotting the local bar were in raptures over Storm's impromptu jam session.

Luca appeared relaxed enough, his foot tapping in time to the music, his arm draped on the booth behind her, but there was an underlying tension about him, as if he regretted making that last comment.

He lived his entire life in the public eye. Was that what he meant, that his life felt like one constant performance? If so, she pitied him. Fame came at a price. She'd seen it many times over the years, rock stars burnt out or strung out, their lives under constant scrutiny, tabloid fodder no matter what they did.

She'd never thought of Luca having to live with the same pressures. When they'd first met she'd painted him as an idle playboy swanking from one end of the globe to another dabbling in charity work but he was so much more than that, had so many facets that she felt guilty for assuming so much.

Luca's hand brushed her shoulder and she smiled, wishing she could apologise for her misconceptions.

'You know, he's not half bad.'

She grinned as Storm serenaded an older couple near the stage, the woman blushing from her wrinkly neck to the roots of her purple-rinse hair. 'Yeah, he can be okay for a miva.'

Luca raised a brow. 'Miva?'

'Male diva.'

He laughed and she quickly averted her gaze before she was swallowed in his dimples whole.

When she studiously kept her gaze fixed on the band, he placed a fingertip under her chin and gently guided her back towards him.

'You know who else isn't half bad when they relax?'

She swallowed at the intent in his eyes, in the open admiration in all that deep blue.

'I'm relaxed all the time,' she said, her breath hitching when his thumb brushed her bottom lip.

'I don't think so.'

He leaned towards her, inching closer until there was nothing but a few millimetres of air between them.

'You're one of the most driven people I've ever seen. Work hours are irrelevant to you. You do what it takes to get the job done. Makes me wonder...'

'What?'

His head edged closer and her heart stuttered.

'Why a gorgeous, intelligent woman like you needs to bury herself in work when she should be relaxing more.'

Oh-oh, now it was her turn to squirm. He'd hit way too close to the mark with that perceptive comment.

Eager to deflect his probing, she tried to ease away from him and failed.

'I relax plenty.'

'Are you relaxed now?'

His lips touched hers in a soft, fleeting kiss that ended before it had begun and had her clamouring for more despite where they were and who could see.

'Relaxation's a state of mind.'

She said the first crazy thing that popped into her head and he laughed, slinging his arm around her shoulder.

'You're one intriguing woman.'

'And you're one irritating man.'

Her soft, breathy sigh at the end of her statement made a mockery of it and he smiled.

'Looks like we have an audience.'

Luca pointed to the stage where Storm launched into a ballad, puckering up in their direction, and she winced. 'So much for professionalism.'

'You're off duty. Don't beat yourself up.'

'Yeah, but I'm supposed to be setting a good example. I'm supposed to be in control...'

She trailed off, knowing exactly why she had to stay in control, increasingly rattled because Luca continued to undermine her protective barriers, getting closer and closer to why this job meant so much to her.

Some of her fear must've shown in her expression for his softened as he backed down, squeezing her shoulder and hugging her close.

'It's okay to lose control sometimes,' he murmured, kissing the top of her head. 'As long as I'm around when you really cut loose.'

Snuggling into his chest, she sighed. Cutting loose around him wasn't the problem. It was regaining control afterwards that would be a killer.

CHAPTER EIGHT

THE moment Charli stepped through the massive red doors leading into the Dragon Museum, peace descended. It had little to do with the soft Chinese music piped in the background or the faint waft of incense and everything to do with the fact Luca had made a detour via the gardens outside.

She needed time away from him.

Whenever she turned around he was there, crowding her space, and for a loner it was more than unsettling.

Yeah, like that was the real reason she needed to get away from him.

Another sell-out crowd last night when the concert had gone off without a hitch, a jam-packed CD signing at Bendigo's largest music store this morning where fans had stretched two blocks to meet Storm, free music lessons with the band for street kids at a local juvenile centre she'd personally pushed for, plus a rock star on his best behaviour.

She should be ecstatic. Instead, ever since that nightcap with Luca during the band's impromptu jam session she'd been on edge. He'd got too close that night, too close to what drove her every day and she couldn't let him in, not when he'd be gone at the end of this tour.

She might be many things; a masochist wasn't one

of them. Luca could flirt and charm her all he liked; she could handle it. What she couldn't handle was the perceptive, multifaceted man who saw a lot more than she gave him credit for.

Scowling, she stepped into the museum, grateful she'd given the entourage the afternoon off, and made straight for Sun Loong, the longest Imperial dragon in the world. His giant head, covered in scales and mirrors and beads, glittered beneath the muted lights, and she craned her head to see his one-hundred-metre body winding upstairs.

She'd always loved dragons as a child, had lost herself in fantasy tales of princes saving princesses from fire-breathing dragons, anything to escape her miserable life.

While Hector wasn't quite the handsome prince she'd envisaged coming along to save her, he was a prince in her eyes, in every way that counted. He'd saved her. She wouldn't be here if it weren't for him and with that sobering thought she started gathering information and writing notes.

'Hard at it?'

She jumped and her pen clattered to the floor as she whirled on Luca. 'You finished already?'

He folded his arms, a wicked grin quirking his lips, lips she remembered in exquisite detail.

'That doesn't sound like you're glad to see me?'

Flustered, and more than a tad annoyed at her rudeness, she picked up her pen and tucked it behind her ear, choosing not to answer his question.

'Are the gardens worth checking out?'

'Yeah, it's a kid's paradise out there. You definitely need to see them before we go.'

'Okay, guess I better get a move on in here, then.'

'Need a hand?'

She needed him to leave her alone so she could concentrate on the task at hand and not be distracted by his crisp lime aftershave, his mesmerising blue eyes and his cheeky smile.

Instead, she found herself nodding. 'That'd be great.'

He rubbed his hands together. 'Good-o. Where do you want me to start?'

Her gaze drifted to his hands, the broad palms, the long, strong fingers, the neat square nails, and as her belly tumbled into a frightening free fall she bit back her first retort of exactly where he could start.

'I'm making a list of the dragons and a few brief points to devise a kind of treasure hunt/quiz for Tiger. Storm and he will only have an hour to pop in here in the morning so I want to make it worthwhile. Maybe you could find the info while I jot it down?'

'Sure.'

Sadly, what she'd thought was a safe pastime to keep him occupied yet far enough away to be comfortable turned into anything but. As they moved between exhibits he dogged her every step, standing way too close, his radiant heat making her fingers tremble as she took notes.

'Wow, check this out,' he said, way too close to her ear for comfort. 'Sun Loong is covered in four-and-a-half thousand scales, ninety thousand mirrors, thirty thousand beads and his head weights twenty-nine kilos. And he was blessed and brought to life by some old dude, one hundred and one years old, dotting his eyes with chicken blood.'

'Ew! Gross.'

His eyes crinkled in amusement at her squeamishness as he patted her arm. 'You're such a girl.'

'Glad you noticed.'

Their gazes locked and she silently cursed for flirting at a time like this. She needed to concentrate and keep a distance, remember? Unfortunately, her memory short-circuited under all that intense blue as a thrill of longing shot through her.

What would it be like to surrender? To give in to the attraction simmering between them? To not second-guess every word, every smile, to just live in the moment and go for it?

'I noticed from the first moment we met.'

His fingertips grazed her hip and she inhaled sharply, overwhelmed and slightly dizzy by his nearness, his masculinity, his everything.

Thoroughly bamboozled, she clutched at her notebook and gripped her pen so hard it almost cracked.

'What about the other dragons in here?'

She half expected him to push the flirting but to her immense relief he turned back to study the wall plaque.

'Along with our friend Sun Loong here, we've got Yar Loong, the night dragon. Then there's Gansu Loong, donated from the Gansu province of China.'

He jerked his thumb over their shoulders and they turned around.

'And this pair are Ming and Ping.'

'Cute,' she said, her pen flying as she took notes. 'What's their story?'

'Ming, with the yellow beard, is the male and means brightness. Ping has the green beard and means peace.'

Typical. Even in the dragon world the female got

dazzled by the male's brightness, leaving her to keep the peace.

He pointed to a small dragon. 'This is Xiao Le Loong, the Little Happy Dragon. And our last is Choi Loong, the newest addition to Bendigo's dragon family.'

She could've listened to his voice all day: smooth, mellifluous, modulated, it lulled her as she wrote and she didn't know what was worse, the fact she could've listened to him all day and night or the fact she wondered what he'd sound like whispering sweet nothings in her ear.

'Apparently he's a competitive dragon, is prosperous, colourful and lucky.'

She was glad someone was getting lucky this trip.

'Great, that's it for this room. I just need to check out the other room where the original Loong is then we're done here.'

He stared at her, an eyebrow raised. 'You're really into this stuff.'

'It's my job.'

'It's more than that and you know it.' He caressed her cheek and she resisted the urge to lean into his hand. 'You get the afternoon off and you choose to come here.'

'I like dragons, always have.'

'It's more than that. You're glowing.'

She shrugged, hating how he did that, saw through her so easily, as if he could peel away her outer layers and see the real her.

'How many people get to do a job they really love? I'm so lucky it's only fair I give it my all.'

He studied her for a long moment and she struggled not to squirm under his scrutiny.

'Come on, let's go check out the oldest Imperial dragon in the world.'

Grateful he bought her distraction, she headed for the room housing an amazing array of ancient artefacts.

'What makes it Imperial?'

'Only the Emporer's dragon has five claws,' she said, her interest sparking anew as they stepped into a huge room filled with engraved wooden screens, exquisite porcelain vases and wax-figure displays.

While the outer room housing the dragons had been impressive in a dazzling, sparkly way, this room had an understated elegance that took her breath away.

'Do you want me to read out the information plaques?'

She shook her head, reluctant to talk and disturb the incredible tranquillity permeating this special place.

'No, thanks. This isn't really a place for kids.'

'But you still want to check it out, huh?'

He touched her hand and that brief touch scared her as much as everything that had come before.

Luca *got* her. He understood how the ambiance of this place affected her and he respected her for it. How could a guy she'd known for less than a week do that? It defied logic. She'd never believed in romance, never believed in love at first sight or soul mates or any of that other crap. But connecting with Luca so quickly, on a deeper level than just physical attraction, scared her.

Living on the streets for a fortnight had been terrifying: avoiding the gangs, the drugs, the pimps, but realising Luca might understand her better than anyone she'd ever met petrified her.

'Go ahead, take your time. I'll wait for you in the gardens.'

He respected her wish to be alone and that raised him

in her esteem even higher. Any higher and his wings would clip the clouds. Or maybe that should be his horns, for as she smiled her thanks he smiled right on back, the familiar, wicked smile that did strange things to her insides.

'Don't be too long though, I want to get you all alone beneath a pagoda.'

Just like that he reverted to his teasing best, reminding her why she could never be serious about a guy like him. A guy here for a fleeting time, a guy who went through life making light of everything, a guy who could never give her the stability she so desperately craved.

Glancing at her watch, she held up her other hand, fingers extended.

'Give me five minutes and I'll meet you outside.'

'Deal.'

He saluted and as he headed back into the main area, faded denim clinging to his long legs like a second skin and accentuating a butt that turned women's heads, she wondered if she could forget all the reasons they shouldn't get together and go for it anyway.

Luca paced the classical Chinese gardens.

He'd already admired the ponds, the fish, the bridges. Now he needed new scenery; namely one stunning blonde who worked far too hard.

He planned to change all that.

Their date a few nights ago had ended badly and while he should be happy he'd succeeded in pushing her away from delving any deeper, for inveigling her way beneath his carefully erected barriers, he wanted to make amends. Wanted to tease the smile back to her face, wanted to make her laugh, wanted her to look at him as if she fancied him as much as he fancied her.

She'd been so serious in the museum and while he admired her dedication his fingers had itched to tug the clip from her hair and send her bun cascading into disarray around her shoulders, to snatch the pen from her fingers, to unbutton her jacket and take a good long hard look at the lacy camisole peeking out beneath.

She liked all that old stuff, he got it, but a part of him wondered if she was deliberately hiding behind her work today, deliberately maintaining her distance after their date.

He'd shut her out over dinner and he'd seen the resulting hurt, her wounded expression. He should be glad she cared about Pop so much she'd suspect his motives but all he could think about was how he'd been irrationally jealous she cared about Pop a hell of a lot more than she cared about him.

Crazy, because he didn't want her to care too much, didn't want her getting too attached or emotionally invested. But for the briefest moment during dinner, when she'd demanded to know why he was really here, he'd wished he had a woman like her to defend him.

His mum never had. She'd only had one primary goal: get Rad to love her back. That, and securing a piece of his fortune. Ironic, she'd never lived to see one of her dreams come true. The trust fund Pop had set up for him had given him a start in life, in the business world that funded his other activities, namely his charities, and he'd never forgotten it.

It was why he was here now; he owed Pop. Guilt was a powerful motivator, and lately, when he schmoozed another half a million out of European royalty or courted a Hollywood A-lister for the publicity it gave to his newest charity, he couldn't ignore the fact he wouldn't be moving in these circles if it weren't for Pop and the start he'd given him.

Pop had done his best over the years to stay in touch, but he'd been obstinate. Not that their occasional catch ups had been anything other than terse and uncomfortable. They had nothing in common, bar Rad—a fact he'd rather forget.

Besides, his gratitude only extended so far and he didn't want Pop getting any ideas: such as he was a replacement for the son he'd lost years ago. Though that wasn't entirely fair. Even when Rad was around Pop had made overtures. Hell, the first time they'd met Pop had been all class. His mum had crashed a Landry family function and when Rad tried to evict them Pop intervened.

He hadn't known about his grandson until that moment, and while Luca had initially been wary of the old man wanting to acknowledge him when his own father didn't, he'd soon realised Hector wasn't Rad and deserved a chance.

As long as Pop didn't make assumptions about why he'd come back now: he was here for the requisite fortnight to repay his debt, that was it. He didn't want to play happy families, didn't want to broach the yawning distance between them. He hadn't gone out of his way over the past decade to initiate contact, tolerating Hector's London stopovers, catching up over snatched lunches, occasionally on the phone.

They had a wary relationship, were acquaintances more than friends. As for family, he didn't know the meaning of the word and that was what scared him, the fact Pop might want to breach the wall of calculated indifference he'd worked so hard on establishing.

'I didn't pick you for the gardening type.'

He turned at Charli's soft voice, something indefinable niggling in his chest. Dismissing it as indigestion after the massive cooked English breakfast he'd consumed, he reached out a hand and snagged hers.

'Put the pen and paper away?'

'I'll store the garden facts up here.' She smiled and tapped her temple. 'Besides, I need some fresh air.'

She glanced around the garden, her eyes widening in appreciation. 'It's beautiful out here.'

'And private.'

She laughed at his exaggerated wink as intended and he tugged on her hand.

'Come on, there's a nice cosy spot beneath that distant pagoda with our name on it...'

Rolling her eyes, she fell into step beside him as they strolled around the small gardens, the rain tumbling in a light sheet. The paved walkways were mostly covered so the drizzle didn't bother them. Though he wouldn't mind slipping off her jacket and seeing what that camisole looked like wet...

Charli liked the rain, liked the freshness of it, liked its symbolism of washing everything clean.

She'd always loved the rain as a kid, had spent hours in it, jumping in puddles and making mud pies and twirling in it. Her mum hadn't cared. The more time she'd spent outside, the better, so Sharon could concentrate on her latest man rather than acknowledge a daughter she wished never had existed.

And it was days like this, when the rain brought the memories flooding back, that she wondered why her mum had her in the first place.

'Whatever's putting that look on your face, stop thinking about it right now or else.'

Forcing a brittle smile, she tilted her head up to look at him.

'Or else what?'

He leaned into her space, his face temptingly close to hers.

'You want to test me?'

Oh, she wanted to do many things with him, testing the least of them.

Pretending to frown, she jabbed him in the chest. 'You don't scare me, big bad Luca Petrelli.'

'No? We'll see about that.'

With a faux growl he lunged at her and she squealed, darting off the path and into the rain.

'Be afraid, be very afraid,' he said, slowing his pace so she remained an arm's length in front of him as she fled, laughing so hard her lungs hurt, eventually stopping and clutching her belly.

'Truce,' she gasped, doubled over, her laughter easing as he caught her, wrapped his arms around her from behind and cradled her against him.

'You think I'll let you get off that easy?'

He spun her around to face him as the last of her giggles faded away, only to be replaced by something much more breath-snatching.

Intense, overwhelming desire.

Raindrops clung to his eyelashes, framing his eyes in crystals, illuminating them and making her want to look into them for ever. And she could've sworn steam rose from between their bodies, their drenched clothes drying from the incredible heat generated between them.

'You can't dare me and get off lightly.'

'Ooh…I'm scared.'

Her shaky laugh faded as his hungry gaze dropped to her lips.

'You should be.'

Before she could respond he swooped in and kissed her. Correction, devoured her, his lips crushing hers in a mind-altering, soul-destroying kiss that changed everything.

She clung to him, her arms wrapped around him in a vice, needing an anchor in a world spinning dangerously out of control.

His tongue danced with hers, a sinuous samba of pleasure as his hands strummed her back, making her ache for more.

All her previous protestations that this thing between them wouldn't go any further evaporated in the steamy summer shower, for nothing was more certain than this kiss was not the end.

It was merely a beginning.

The door to the apartment crashed open as they tumbled through it, mouths melded, hands frantic, oblivious to everything bar quenching their hunger for each other.

Charli couldn't remember the five-minute drive from the museum to the apartment, couldn't remember the itinerary for this afternoon, couldn't remember anything but how Luca tasted and smelled and felt.

He pushed her up against the wall and kicked the door shut, his body heat warming her better than a hot shower.

'Better get you out of these wet clothes,' he murmured in her ear, nipping the lobe, sucking it into his mouth and tonguing it 'til she groaned.

'Can't wait that long,' she gasped out, popping the button on his jeans and sliding the zip down in one fluid movement.

He stilled and she inwardly screamed, *No, no, no, don't you dare stop.*

Raising his head, he looked her straight in the eye. 'You sure you want this?'

'Does this answer your question?'

Sliding her hands under the waistband of his jeans, she eased them down over his hips and touched her pelvis to his.

He groaned. 'No regrets afterwards. No second-guessing. No—'

'You talk too much.'

She kissed him, showing him exactly how much she wanted this.

Now.

Thankfully, he shelved his gallantry and went for it, tugging on zips and popping buttons and ripping a camisole along the way to getting her naked.

'Bedroom,' he muttered, shucking his jeans and jocks in a co-ordinated move that would put a stripper to shame, and managing to protect himself without breaking lip contact.

'Here. Now.'

She wrapped a leg around his thigh and her arms around his neck, whimpering when he lifted her waist, rubbed along her moist core once, twice, before sliding in to the hilt.

She should've questioned the sanity of this, should've had some reservations, should've done a thousand and one things not involving getting hot, naked and sweaty with Luca Petrelli but she'd lost the will to think when he'd kissed her in the rain. And had no intention of getting rational now.

As he thrust into her, harder and deeper and faster, driving her closer to the edge, driving her insane with wanting him, she gave over to the heat spiralling from the inside out, the growing tension, the exquisite pleasure bordering on pain as he drove her higher.

She plunged over the edge with a scream, burying her face in the crook of his neck, biting down on his shoulder.

He roared, driving hard one last time before shattering along with her.

Stunned and sated she clung to him, her head lolling back against the wall, her legs wrapped around his waist, anchoring him inside her.

She didn't want this intimacy to end, didn't want to deal with the aftermath or the inevitable awkwardness.

With the few times she'd had sex in the past, she'd quickly dressed and exited, not wanting to build false hopes; the guys she'd briefly dated hadn't come close to what she'd been looking for.

This time, there was no escape.

'Stop thinking so much,' he said, lifting his head off her shoulder, his crooked grin slamming into her heart with the force of an electric-guitar rip.

Her *heart*?

Hell.

'I'm not.'

'Yeah?'

He massaged her temple, his pressure so light it bordered on sensual. 'I can feel those cogs turning.'

'Only one thing for it, then,' she said, hating how her voice quivered, hating how her well-protected heart trembled more. 'Distract me.'

'My pleasure.'

And as he carried her to the shower, followed by the bed much later, he did.

Over and over again. All afternoon.

CHAPTER NINE

CHARLI dealt in cold, hard facts.

At work she double-checked travel itineraries, tour dates, stage bookings, launch parties, security staff, ensuring everything ran smoothly and leaving no room for mistakes.

So what the hell was her excuse for the monumental mistake she'd just made?

As Luca rolled over in bed, propped on an elbow and grinned, she was looking straight at him.

The white sheet draped over his waist, tangled in his legs, leaving him deliciously naked from the waist up, his beautiful bronze torso scoured with nail marks.

God, she'd been mad for him. Insatiable. Unable to get enough. How many times had they made love since he'd taken her up against the wall? Three? Five? More?

She'd lost count after her first three screaming orgasms, had been completely and delightfully out of it.

Then in the bathtub, after he'd lathered handmade lavender soap all over her body, massaged her scalp until she'd whimpered and toyed with her until she'd orgasmed—three times in a row—she'd been mindless and she'd made her mistake.

When he'd wrapped a fluffy bath towel around her, scooped her into his arms, carried her to the bed, laid

her on it, unwrapped her like the best present he'd ever
received and made mad, passionate love to her, she'd
tipped over the edge. And not just metaphorically.

Before the bathtub, they'd had sex.

Afterwards, they'd made love and for her that was a
huge distinction. And a huge mistake.

She'd let him *in*, into a place in her heart no one ever
ventured, and it terrified her.

It hadn't registered at the time or later, when they'd
curled up together and passed out for a good two hours,
but now...

'Oh-oh. You've got that look.'

She nibbled on her bottom lip, shuffling from one foot
to another, wondering how fast she could do a runner.

'What look?'

'The old now-that-the-fun's-over-how-fast-can-I-
get-away? look.'

Damn, he was good.

'I'm not going anywhere.'

Considering they were sharing this apartment, where
could she run to anyway?

She padded over to the bed, remained standing. If
she sat and he reached for her again, she doubted she'd
have the will power to resist.

'Think I'll go for a walk.'

His endearingly crooked smile faded. 'Now?'

'Yeah, clear my head.'

He sat up, all trace of teasing gone.

'What's wrong?'

Inwardly wincing, she took a deep breath and settled
for the direct approach.

'This afternoon was incredible but we should concentrate on work for the rest of the tour.'

Swiping a hand over his face didn't erase the tension. 'We should, huh?'

She blushed and shuffled her feet. 'Yeah, it's for the best. We're adults, we can continue working together, what just happened shouldn't be a problem.'

But there was a problem, a big one, for the guy she'd let creep under her guard, the guy she'd just made love to many times, the guy she thought was noble and charming and deeper than she first thought, was now staring at her as if she'd tarnished the incredible afternoon they'd shared.

She stood there, wringing her hands until she realised what she was doing and tucked them into the robe's deep pockets, waiting for him to say something, anything, to make this situation better.

For once, the guy who hadn't shut up since they'd met remained scarily silent, a frown slashing his brow, his sensual lips pinched.

It wasn't as if there was any chance of a future for them so this was for the best. The second she'd realised she'd made love was the second she knew Luca had broached her carefully erected defences. She had to shut him out. She had to. A repeat of this afternoon would only lead to one thing: a one-way trip down heartbreak highway.

'I think it's for the best.'

'You're right.'

She quickly averted her gaze as he stood and wrapped the top sheet around his waist. Not that she hadn't already seen everything and, boy, had it been impressive.

Not a good thought at this stage of proceedings because her face flushed at the memory, weakening her resolve.

If he were a different guy, if she were a stronger girl...

what would it be like to take a chance on a real relationship with a guy like Luca?

'Yeah, we need to concentrate on work.' He hitched the sheet higher and padded towards the bathroom. 'That's the great thing about flings. Once it's out of your system it's easy to get back to the important stuff.'

She froze, her deliberate blasé act splintering into a million painful fragments that lodged in her heart and drove home the insidious, unwelcome truth.

That while she'd fallen for him during their deliriously special, life-altering encounter a few hours earlier, he'd seen it as nothing more than a fling.

And all the rationale in the world urging her to push him away before he got any closer counted for nothing in the face of his callous indifference.

Luca went through the process of showering and dressing on autopilot. He shaved like a robot, nicking under his chin twice and not noticing until blood dripped into the basin. Watching it trickle down the side and slide into the hole, he wondered if it was a sign.

Thanks to his stupidity, his life could be down the plughole too.

He'd labelled what they'd shared as a fling...

Slamming a fist into the wall, he barely registered the pain. Could he be any more of a bastard?

He stared at his stricken face in the mirror, the shame in his eyes, the worry lines that had sprung up almost instantaneously. He never wanted to get emotionally involved with anyone, had taken great steps to ensure it wouldn't happen over the years.

Then Charli had come along, creeping under his guard, making him mad with wanting her. And he'd had her, over and over again... What had happened in that bathtub... Just thinking about it made him hard and he turned away from the mirror in disgust. He had more important things to worry about right now than his libido.

Like how he could make it up to Charli.

She'd caught him off guard, giving him the brush-off after the amazing afternoon they'd had. They'd connected on so many levels, getting physical merely cemented what he knew: they were great together.

He'd had it all worked out in his head: spend the rest of his time here burning up the sheets together, having fun together, enjoying it while it lasted. Never in his wildest dreams had he expected her to give him the 'thanks but no thanks' speech before their passion had barely cooled.

He'd been surprised, rattled and increasingly annoyed in that order, resulting in that throwaway remark about flings and getting this thing between them out of their systems.

He should've been happy to re-establish the status quo, to ensure there were no feelings involved, to clear up any possible misconceptions that what they'd shared had been nothing but steamy sex.

But he'd seen the hurt in her eyes and had instantly wished he could erase those few minutes and go back to the two of them wrapped in each other's arms.

Logically, what had happened was for the best.

So how could he explain away the uncharacteristic twinge of remorse insisting it was anything but?

Charli did a last-minute check on her to-do list as Luca slid into the driver's seat to drive to a nearby winery where Storm was doing a twilight concert.

Not that she needed to. She'd checked the list a hundred times already, anything to keep her mind off the disastrous way the best afternoon of her life had ended.

When Luca had come out of the bathroom he'd been business as usual, acting as if their afternoon of passion and the fallout had never happened.

She should've been glad. They had a ton of work to do before the 'Storming the Vines' concert tonight, a welcome distraction from the underlying awkwardness between them, yet between making calls to the winery and jotting down last-minute to-do lists she snuck surreptitious peeks at him, wishing things could be different before mentally kicking herself.

If anything, the aftermath of their blissful afternoon had reinforced she'd be a fool to let him creep under her guard.

As Luca eased the car out of the car park of the apartments, the images of a few hours ago slammed into her memory: unable to keep their hands off each other in the car, practically falling up the steps, fumbling with the door key, flinging the door open to tumble into each other's arms.

She'd wanted him so badly, had been mad for him. A madness that had bubbled away under the surface all afternoon, a madness that resulted in her feeling like this. Confused. Dazed. Torn. For while she could logically tell herself she could never fall for a guy like him, what if it was already too late?

She risked a quick glance at his profile, her heart turning over. Yep, no doubt about it. For all her self-talk and rational arguments, she was in serious danger of falling for a guy guaranteed to break her heavily guarded heart.

'Concert itinerary all set?'

'Yeah, ready to go,' she said, the conversation petering out that quickly.

She hated this, hated how awkward they'd become around each other when a few hours ago they'd been closeted in intimacy that shut out the rest of the world, cocooning them in a fantasy.

Sadly, fantasies were just that—make-believe, daydreams—and she should know better than anyone that all the wishing in the world didn't bring you what you wanted most. She'd tried growing up, boy, had she tried: wishing for a mum to love her, a nice place to live, a room that didn't have mould on the cornices and roaches scuttling the floor at night.

Wishing got her nowhere, which was why she made things happen. Pity she couldn't make the sparks and fun and heat they'd shared a few hours ago return, without the fear of her falling harder and minus a guy who viewed her as just another fling.

'Look, Charli, about before—'

'Don't worry about it, all dealt with, moving on.'

'Moving on?'

'Concentrating on the important stuff, like finishing this country tour and gearing up for the Melbourne show next week.'

'And us?'

Her silence spoke volumes and he indicated, pulled off the highway, spraying gravel as he braked.

'I hate this.'

He thumped the steering wheel, a frustration she understood all too well radiating off him.

Swiping a hand over his face, he swivelled towards her. 'We were getting along really well and now you can barely look at me.'

Not for the reason he thought. She wasn't angry about

his flippant fling comment. No, the reason she couldn't look at him was for fear he'd see right through her, would know that she'd allowed him into her heart as well as her body.

For a few incredible days she'd had a glimpse of what it was like to be wanted by a man, to be lavished with attention, to be on the receiving end of genuine charm. And she'd revelled in it, had blossomed into a woman confident in her appeal, a woman who knew what she wanted and wasn't afraid to get it, a woman who had incredible, mind-altering afternoon sex with a man she'd known for less than a week.

A woman who faced her fear and did it anyway. So why was she acting like a coward now?

'It's not you. I just don't know what to say.'

He captured her hand and the sizzle of heat surprised her. She thought it might have waned after they consummated their relationship; if anything, the buzz between them had intensified.

'Maybe we don't have to say anything. Maybe we try and go back to how things were before we, uh…lost the plot.'

'You honestly think we can?'

His lopsided smile twanged her heart.

'Worth a try.'

Lifting her hand, he brushed a kiss across the back of it and she sighed. Her pulse skipped through her veins, a reminder of how badly she'd like to renege on her previous stance and throw herself wholeheartedly into this *fling*. But she couldn't do it, not when she knew it had moved beyond flirting for her, that she might actually care for him. No point getting in any deeper when he'd be out of her life in a week.

She wriggled her hand out of his and tapped her watch.

'Right now, we've got a job to do and I need you to get me to that winery to do it.'

He searched her face—for the truth behind her reticence? For a sign she still wanted him?—before nodding.

'Fine, I'll let you off the hook.'

As he started the engine, glanced over his shoulder and pulled back onto the highway he added, 'For now.'

Charli had organised several twilight concerts at wineries in the Yarra Valley just out of Melbourne, loved the informality of families sitting on picnic rugs, loved the wine tastings, loved the relaxed ambiance.

She'd had her doubts about Storm pulling off something like this—his whole snarky demeanour suited dark stages and pubs—but as he crooned out his last song, a ballad from his early days, she finally slumped onto a stool and took her first sip of a divine chardonnay.

'He's done well.'

A shiver shimmied down her spine as Luca pulled up a stool next to her, thigh-touching, arm-rubbing close.

'Yeah, better than I expected.'

'Yet you played the supremely confident role extremely well the last week.' His admiration sent a flush of warmth through her. 'Had me fooled.'

Yeah, she was good at that. She'd even fooled herself into believing nothing existed between them beyond a bit of harmless flirting.

'Ready to head back to the apartment?'

Downing the rest of her wine in three gulps, she

shook her head. 'Actually, there's been a change of plan. We're driving to Echuca tonight.'

He frowned. 'Tonight?'

'Yeah, we've only got a few hours there in the morning with Storm's signing and Tiger wanted to ride the paddle steamers too, so better if we head up there tonight and get an early start.'

All sounded very logical and Tiger really did want to take a ride on a paddle steamer, but the main motivating force for not spending another night in Bendigo was the fact she couldn't face spending a night in the apartment with Luca.

The way she was feeling—in over her head, emotional, floundering—she'd rather take her chances in Storm's bus!

Thankfully she'd rung ahead to Echuca during the concert and double-checked the booking for separate apartments, ensuring there were no natural disasters or other catastrophes that she had failed to hear about.

'How far is it?'

'About seventy minutes—a cruisy drive.'

'Uh-huh.'

Wanting to get the rest out before she lost her nerve, she cleared her throat. 'If you could drive my car, that'd be great, because I have some logistical stuff to run through with Storm.'

If she didn't feel so lousy at fobbing him off, his raised eyebrows would've been comical.

'You're riding in the bus?'

His disbelief made it sound as if she were hitchhiking a ride to Mars.

'Yeah, it's the only comfortable place we can spread out the paperwork we need to go over.'

'Right. Paperwork.'

A frown slashed his brow, his compressed lips a dead giveaway he was trying to hold back what he really thought of the new travel arrangements.

Eager to make her escape while the going was good, she slid off the stool and gathered up her work stuff. 'Thanks, Luca, I knew you'd understand.'

Only problem was, she didn't understand any of this, least of all how her heart seemed to be breaking just by walking away from him now.

Charli couldn't do this any more. If she'd reached her limit yesterday, today had pushed her over the edge.

To her immense relief, Storm had been the model rock star: no tantrums, no come-ons, no crap—and that had just been on the bus last night. And this morning he'd breezed through another photo promo and CD-signing for local fans, wowing Echuca as he had Ballarat and Bendigo.

She couldn't fault his work ethic since the unfortunate wine-bar incident and the fact they'd be heading back to Melbourne on a high that boded well for the upcoming concert.

No, Storm wasn't the problem. But playing the good little tour manager right to the end was, and that meant she'd accompanied Storm and Tiger, with Luca tagging along, as they'd spent a few hours on a Murray River cruise, strolled through Moama market admiring the local crafts, tasting the local produce, all very touristy and laid-back and a good wind down after the hectic pace of the past week.

The major problem had come when she'd had to hang out with Luca and pretend the underlying tension between them didn't exist. But it was there all the same, intangible yet ever-present, a taut wire ready to snap.

'Have another scone?'

Luca pushed the plate towards her and she patted her tummy. 'Thanks, but I'm done.'

A sign of how truly rattled she was, that she couldn't squeeze in another of the best scones in the world served at the cosy Wistaria café. Back in Melbourne she could scoff two without blinking and the Devonshire tea served there wasn't a patch on this.

If he sensed her reticence he didn't show it. 'What's on the agenda when we get back to Melbourne?'

Anything, as long as it didn't involve spending time with him.

'Collating a final report on the tour. Preparing for the Melbourne concert.'

He rested his forearms on the table and leaned towards her, the knowing glint in his eyes alerting her to the fact he was far more astute than she gave him credit for.

'If I didn't know any better I'd say you're trying to get away from me.'

So much for subtlety. Deliberately relaxing into her chair, she shook her head.

'It's what I always do; collate everything on the last day so I can hit the office running tomorrow.'

'Pop's a slavedriver, huh?'

'Hector's a fair boss, always has been.'

'Loyalty, I like that.'

She fidgeted with the edge of a lacy tablecloth, desperate to escape. She didn't want to talk about her job or Hector or the music business. She needed to get away before it was too late and she fell under his spell just a little bit more.

Would Luca be so nonchalant if he knew the truth?

Would he want to sit here if he knew how much she cared, if he knew she was in too deep? She doubted it.

'Let's go.'

She sounded abrupt but couldn't sit here another second longer and, standing, she grabbed her bag.

'Hey, slow down.'

He snagged her arm and she stiffened, hating it had come to this. A few days ago she'd yearned for his touch, would've melted at the briefest brush of his fingers. Now, his strong fingers wrapped around her forearm elicited a host of memories leading to one thing: she might be in love with a guy so totally wrong for her.

Ironic, she'd spent years trying to prove how different she was from her mother and in the end they might be more alike than she'd thought.

Falling for the wrong guy.

Depending on that guy for her happiness.

Hells bells.

'Sorry, I really have to go.'

She yanked her arm free, ready to bolt when he stood.

'Charli, this is crazy—'

She fled without looking back.

After his twentieth circuit of the old historic port, Luca knew he had to do something. Walking hadn't taken the edge off and he'd explode if he didn't head back to the apartments now and confront Charli.

Though what was he going to say?

I'm sorry things ended this way?

I'm sorry for starting this in the first place?

I'm sorry for hurting you?

Because she *was* hurting. He could see it in her

tense shoulders, in her pinched mouth, in the haunting emptiness in her eyes whenever she glanced his way.

That was what killed him the most, the fact she could barely look at him any more when they'd shared so many emotion-laden, spark-worthy, loaded stares before. She had the most beautiful green eyes he'd ever seen, the colour of the ocean off Nice on a summer's day...

Sheesh, where was he getting this stuff? Must be turning soft. Had to be Charli's fault. She brought out that side of him, made him want to be a better man when he was with her.

Pop was like that: old school, gallant. Luca liked to think he'd inherited some of his chivalry, the part that had bypassed his father.

Something twinged painfully in his chest, a stab of regret for what might have been if he hadn't been so stubborn all these years and let Pop into his life more.

They'd spoken regularly on this tour, mainly business, and he admired the old guy, liked his sense of humour, his vibrancy, his no-bull attitude. If he hadn't harboured so much resentment towards Rad maybe he could've had a closer relationship with Pop?

Damn Rad, damn him to hell for influencing his life despite how much he'd done to ensure the contrary. Even now, the way he'd botched things with Charli, it all came back to his past and how he struggled to emotionally connect with anyone. Which he'd liked just fine.

Until now.

He rubbed his chest, blinked and glanced around, surprised to find himself standing in the main street of Echuca. He'd never been a daydreamer—no point in imagining things that would never happen, his childhood had been testament to that—but everything about the past week, from teasing a smile out of Charli to sweeping her into his arms, had him fantasising about things he'd never considered.

A future.

With her.

Crazy, for a guy whose longest relationship consisted of a fortnight's wining and dining, but there was something special about Charli and the way she lit up his life that prompted him to do something completely out of character and stick around for a while.

For how long? And what about his work? The charities? Her job? The logistics?

No, even contemplating spending more than another week in Melbourne had his head spinning. Which begged the question: apart from overseeing the finances for the rest of the tour, how *would* he spend his remaining time in Melbourne?

He knew what he'd like: to recapture the old magic with Charli and have a whoop-up time before he headed back to his well-ordered, well-structured life in London. But that would be tantamount to flinging himself off the top of a cliff without a tethering bungee rope.

He couldn't risk it. If she already had him thinking beyond the next week, he'd already slipped up and allowed her to get too close.

Rather than contemplating spending time with her—yeah, as if she'd really go for that after the past few days—he should be concentrating on winding work up and heading back to London.

Yeah, that was what he'd do. Keep things platonic with Charli, finish up his financial duties and repay his debt to Pop, and head back to his well-ordered, well-structured life.

Easy.

The moment that one little word popped into his head,

he remembered the way Charli had looked dripping wet in the Chinese Gardens, the way she'd matched him step for step as they'd crashed through that door into the apartment, the way she'd come apart in his arms repeatedly all afternoon, and he knew staying away from her over the next week would be anything but easy.

CHAPTER TEN

'WHAT are you doing here?'

Charli jumped as Hector strode into her office, beaming smile welcoming. She wondered how long it'd last when he heard she'd snubbed his grandson and had every intention of maintaining her indifference during the rest of his stay in Melbourne.

It was the only way. She couldn't afford to get any more involved than she already was.

'The country tour was a bigger hit than we anticipated and I've got loads more to do to make sure we're on top of the Melbourne concert.'

He studied her with the same gentle yet astute gaze he'd used since he'd found her squatting in his shed ten years ago.

'Luca too much for you to handle?'

She blushed, silently cursing her reaction.

'He wasn't too bad.'

Hector guffawed. 'Now I know you're lying.'

He took a seat on the other side of her desk and she gnawed on her bottom lip, unprepared for this.

She hadn't expected Hector to be here: she'd checked his schedule to make sure. But now he was she'd be forced to discuss the road trip and hope to God her face wouldn't give away the truth.

'I've heard my grandson's exuberance results in one of two outcomes. You either love him or hate him.'

With a wink, Hector rested his forearms on her desk. 'So which was it for you, Charlotte?'

Much to her chagrin, her blush intensified.

'Neither. We got on well enough.'

Well enough for two people who had been instantly attracted and couldn't keep their hands off each other.

If Hector saw something beneath her glib response, he didn't push.

'Storm behaved?'

'Mostly.'

'And his kid?'

'Tiger had a ball. Panned for gold, travelled deep into an underground mine and wouldn't get off the paddle steamer.'

Hector's eyes lit up. 'I might have to supervise the next country tour personally.'

She chuckled at his enthusiasm. 'Men never grow up.'

'Oh, I don't know about that. Luca has done a fine job.'

Yeah, she could attest to that for the most part. But while Luca might be grown up, part of him was like her, damaged by his upbringing. She got that now, had pondered it at great length on her three-hour trip back from Echuca when Storm had grown tired of discussing business and retired to play on the Wii with Tiger.

If she was scared of letting anyone under her guard, Luca must be the same. He was involved in all those projects, funded kids' charities the world over...but how invested was he really? Did he just dole out money or did he get involved? The way he'd dismissed their beautiful encounter as nothing more than a fling, she had a feeling he never, ever got involved, with anything or anybody.

Despite her best efforts to maintain an impartial expression, some of her doubt must've shown.

'He's very clever, cultivating his image in the media to keep his charities in the spotlight.'

Yes, but what had he said... Something about performing becoming tiring after a while...?

She'd initially taken him for a shallow playboy, had had her misconceptions blown away early when he'd started to reveal pieces of himself. So what would it be like, to have to *perform* all the time? She saw the toll it took on rock stars. What toll had it taken on Luca?

'From kids with cancer to the homeless, he gives millions. I've always been proud of that boy.'

Then why hadn't he said so? Apart from the occasional mention of Luca in a magazine, Hector rarely talked about his grandson. And after seeing the way the two talked on the phone, their relationship was strained at best.

Was it Luca's fault, not wanting to get involved with anyone, including his grandfather? In a small way, it should give her comfort; it wasn't only her Luca didn't want to get involved with, it was people in general.

Had his upbringing scarred him that much? Considering her childhood had been no walk in the park she understood but it didn't make their situation any easier. She'd fallen for a guy who wouldn't know emotion from an electric guitar.

'Admirable,' she said, increasingly uncomfortable with discussing Saint Luca with his grandfather when Hector flipped open his wallet and slid it across the desk, surprising her further.

'My grandson is something.'

Stunned that Hector carried around a picture of Luca in his wallet, she glanced at the picture of Luca in a graduation cap and gown, his smile forced while Hector grinned with pride, his arm looped around Luca's shoulders. The two were so much alike she was surprised she hadn't spotted the similarities sooner: the strong nose, the cut-glass cheekbones, the squarish jaw.

'When was this taken?'

'Twelve years ago.'

She didn't understand why he was showing her this now. Strangely enough, it hurt. They were more than boss and employee, mentor and protégé. Hector was like family and she wished she'd known more about Luca before now.

Why? So she wouldn't have fallen for him?

Sadly, she had a suspicion no amount of pre-warning could've prevented that.

'You're wondering why I've never discussed Luca with you?'

She opened her mouth to fib and found she couldn't. Hector was the father she'd never had and she couldn't lie to him.

'A little.'

Hector's wistful gaze as he stared at the picture in his wallet brought a lump to her throat.

'Because there's not much to talk about. We're not close.'

'Not for lack of trying on your part, I bet,' she muttered, suddenly angry at the emotionally closed-off man she'd grown to like way more than was good for her.

Hector snapped the wallet shut and slid it back into his pocket. 'Too little too late, I fear.'

What did he mean by that? From what Luca had told her, Hector had acknowledged him the moment he'd discovered he existed. He'd paid for his education, he'd attended his graduation from that picture, he'd called him for help now.

She wanted to ask what he meant but took one look at his shuttered expression and clamped her lips.

'I wanted us to be closer but I didn't know how,' he murmured, so softly she barely heard, a lump in her throat forming at his audible regret.

'We go through the motions of catching up now and then but we've never really bonded.'

That sounded like Luca: mindful of the one person who'd given him a start in life yet not wanting to get too close.

'I wish things could be different.'

Swallowing past the lump in her throat, she said, 'Have you told him that?'

Hector pinched the bridge of his nose, looking every inch his seventy-plus years.

'Not really. We're both as bad as each other, skirting around the important stuff.'

He rubbed at the weary frown between his brows. 'Rad treated that boy appallingly and I wanted to make up for it. But...'

She knew what he was going to say. *'But by then it was too late.'* Luca had already erected his emotional barriers, had learned to trust no one.

Her heart ached for the impressionable boy he must've been, a boy who had to watch his mother throw away her life over a man who didn't love her, a boy who had to endure his father rejecting him many times over, a boy who was too scared, too emotionally bruised, to trust any overture from a grandfather he was too scared to get to know.

'Luca cares about you. He wouldn't be here otherwise.'

His face softened as he patted her hand where it lay on the desk, gripping the mouse.

'I hope so. You can't blame an old man for getting sentimental in his dotage and wishing things were different.'

Charli wanted to offer him platitudes. She wanted to say that Luca did care, that in helping his grandfather out of a tight spot he might be opening the door to a closer relationship.

Instead, she kept her mouth shut, for while she hoped those things were true how well did she really know Luca? She'd thought she was starting to, then he'd slammed up that invisible wall after they had sex—a wall she'd wanted and actively encouraged yet that didn't make it any easier—and it had left her wondering ever since.

'I'll let you get back to work. Just because our resident ornery star behaved himself on the first leg of the tour, doesn't mean he won't throw a tantrum if the rest isn't perfectly scheduled.'

'Good point.'

Hector paused at the door, the wrinkles at the corners of his eyes deepening with mischief.

'Getting to know my grandson is worth the effort. Give him a chance.'

Speechless, she ducked behind her PC screen, not wanting him to see yet another incriminating blush.

CHAPTER ELEVEN

CHARLI stiffened as her mobile rang. She didn't have to glance at caller ID to know who it was. In fact, she'd expected Luca to call sooner, around the time she'd run out of the café in Echuca without looking back.

Though she'd mentally rehearsed a hundred responses, every single one deserted her as she flipped the phone from hand to hand like a hot potato.

She had to stay firm on her decision to keep things strictly professional between them. He'd be sticking around Landry Records for the next week, seeing this tour through to the end, which meant she'd be seeing him daily, bearing the brunt of his potent charm.

Steadying her resolve to distance herself, she pressed the answer button with a shaky thumb.

'Hey, Luca.'

'If it isn't the great Houdini.'

Glad he could see humour in the situation, she clenched the phone to her ear.

'It wasn't so much a disappearing act as a dash of mercy.'

'For who?'

'Me. Storm. We had a ton of tour stuff to go through and having his uninterrupted attention for more than five minutes was too good an opportunity to pass up.'

His loaded silence didn't bode well.

'Dedication I can understand. Ditching me to be holed up in Storm's tour bus, again, for three hours? Confusing the hell out of me.'

'I told you, it was work—'

'Cut the bull.'

His exasperated huff sliced through the taut silence. 'I thought we'd dealt with what happened in Bendigo.'

She froze, her blood chill and sluggish as it slithered through her veins. She didn't want to discuss this, didn't want him probing for answers she wasn't willing to give. Besides, she knew if he ever found out she was in deeper than he thought it wouldn't just affect their working relationship over the next week, it might affect his relationship with Hector too.

And how happy would her boss be if she ran off his grandson before they'd got to spend more time together, as he obviously craved?

'Look, things happened so quickly between us I just felt out of control. Like I was sucked up in a vortex and thrown around.'

She stopped toying with a pen and flung it on the desk, knowing she'd have to give him some semblance of the truth before she blew it completely.

'I just needed some down time and a three-hour car ride together would've been too—too—'

'Cosy?'

'*Claustrophobic* is the word I was looking for.'

He *tsk-tsked*. 'Charli, Charli, Charli, when are you going to admit it?'

'Admit what?'

'That you're crazy about me.'

She snorted. 'Like the rest of the world's female population?'

'Jealous?'

'What do you think?'

He paused and longing shimmied through her. She *was* crazy about him, on the verge of making a catastrophic mistake and falling head over heels in love if she lost her battle with herself.

But she couldn't do it. She wasn't her mum and she'd be damned if she was foolish enough to hand her heart to a footloose, fancy-free playboy who'd squash it completely when he headed back to his jet-set life.

'I get it. Things happened pretty fast between us. You're scared. Not that I blame you.'

He cleared his throat, his nervousness surprising her. 'I'm a flake, Charli. I'll woo you and charm you and you'll have the time of your life but I can't make any promises.'

'I know,' she murmured, horrified when her breath caught and it sounded like a stifled sob.

A strange sound filtered through the phone, as if he was twirling a pen in his fingers and tapping it against a desk; couldn't be, for that would mean he was as anxious as she was.

Throw in the fact she'd never heard that serious undertone in his voice let alone seen the confident charmer be anything less than assured and she knew his edginess matched hers.

'But you intrigue me, you captivate me, you make me want to slay dragons and dig with my bare hands to find you the biggest gold nugget on the planet.'

He paused, dragged in a breath that sounded as ragged as hers. 'I know this sounds crazy because I'm gone in a week and things are super awkward between us at the moment but do you want to go for broke? See this through to the end?'

Tears stung her eyes and she blinked them back. He'd been so brutally honest whereas she hid behind half-truths and fear. That constant, ever-present fear that if she truly let go and depended on another person to be happy, she'd end up destitute.

Not in the same way she'd once been, facing down sleazy pimps, drugged-out prostitutes and feral street kids as a teenager living on the streets, but emotionally destitute, and that would be far, far worse.

'Charli?'

Her heart twisted with regret as she swiped away the silent tears trickling down her cheeks.

'Sorry, I can't.'

She hit the disconnect button, the mobile falling from her lifeless fingers as she knuckled her eyes, finally letting the soul-racking sobs come.

It had been the worst week of Charli's life.

Refusing to indulge in a wild, passionate, no-holds-barred fling with Luca had been the smartest thing she could've possibly done. And the most painful.

Where work had once been her haven it was now a place of forced formalities and polite small-talk and pretending. They both tiptoed around each other, discussing work and little else, her rebuttal of Luca's offer the elephant in the room every time they crossed paths.

Every minute of every day was pure, bamboo-under-her-fingernails torture.

While there was never any doubt she'd ever be anything than one-hundred-per-cent professional, seeing this tour through to the end had drained her to the point of exhaustion. During Storm's down time, she'd accompanied him and his entourage to the small jazz bars dotting Melbourne's laneways, to a vibrant Broadway stage show, to exquisite restaurants from lavish five-star French to tiny five-table Vietnamese cafés.

They'd strolled along the boardwalk at Williamstown and sipped lattes on cake-heaven Acland Street, Storm and the band lapping up the new stardom a resurrected rock career brought while she stayed in the background, playing the diligent tour manager always on the lookout for trouble.

And trouble she found, every single day, for Luca accompanied them on every outing, an ever-present reminder of what she wanted yet couldn't have.

Sure, he had a legitimate reason for being there, taking his role looking after the finances seriously but it was more than that and she knew it. He had another agenda. To slowly but surely drive her insane.

Maybe he thought she'd crumble if he was in her face twenty-four-seven? Maybe he had full confidence she'd crack beneath the onslaught of his impressive charms?

Okay, so she was being excessively harsh. Luca couldn't help who he was—attractive, outgoing, charismatic—and in fairness to him, he hadn't been flirting with her. In fact, he appeared to loathe their encounters as much as she did, discomfited by their gauche, inept conversations where before there'd been teasing and laughter and light.

Whatever his motivation she couldn't stand another minute of it and despite her rigid determination to hold him at bay, to try to eradicate that one incredible afternoon she'd spent in his arms from her memory, she couldn't forget.

She knew it was foolish, knew it with every resistant cell in her body but spending all her time with Luca, albeit on a professional level, had her feeling more alive than she'd ever been.

Was this how her mum had felt with her guys? This all-consuming, overwhelming need to be with that person?

Not that it excused Sharon's appalling lack of maternal care but it went some way to explaining her horrid behaviour.

How many times over the years had she watched her mum preen for some guy, watched her glow with excitement and blossom under a little male attention? And while she wasn't that bad she knew deep down, in a place she'd deliberately shut off from Luca the moment she realised she was getting in over her head, she lapped up every bit of his attention the way her mum had with her suitors.

With a groan, she glanced at her watch. Now wasn't the time for self-analysis. Luca would be here soon and she had less than ten minutes to dress and put the finishing touches on her make-up.

Officially, they were attending the Arias, Australia's big music-industry awards, in support of Storm on a professional level.

Unofficially, Luca had caught her at a weak moment and she'd agreed to let him pick her up despite wanting to ensure tonight was about work. Hector had been around when he'd asked how she was getting to the awards so she'd had no choice but to agree to his offer.

But that was where it ended. The guy was leaving in two days and, while the Arias were always fabulously glamorous and had an after-party that had to be seen to be believed, she had to ensure Luca didn't get the wrong idea about her letting him squire her along the red carpet.

Slipping into the floor-length gold-sequinned sheath and matching strappy sandals, she twirled in front of the mirror. Not bad. The side split to mid-thigh revealed a fair bit of leg and the bodice hugged her curves, giving the illusion of a bigger bust.

A killer dress, to match her killer resolve.

She couldn't let Luca see how much she was looking forward to tonight, couldn't let him see beneath her carefully controlled mask.

Two more days… Not too hard to survive, surely?

The doorbell rang and her tummy tumbled with nervous anticipation. Taking a deep breath to quell her nerves, she opened the door and her tummy dropped away again.

She'd seen Luca Petrelli in casual denim, formal chic and, her personal favourite, naked. But Luca in a designer tux, his caramel curls slicked back, blue eyes dark with excitement, made her heart expand until she could barely breathe.

'You're stunning.'

'Thanks.'

He stood on the threshold, uncertain, his expression torn between wariness and hope.

She didn't want to encourage him, didn't want to give him the wrong idea, but the fact this gorgeous, confident man almost squirmed under the weight of her rejection hit home hard and made her feel more than a tad guilty.

Wanting to ease the tension, at least for tonight, she smiled, putting her heart and soul into it, and the result was a spectacular transformation that wiped the guardedness from his face and replaced it with cautious optimism.

'Let's just have fun tonight, okay?'

Maybe she shouldn't have said *fun* because he took hold of her hand, twirled her out before reeling her into his arms where he crushed her to him. Caught off guard, she stared at him, speechless, a second before his mouth claimed hers in a sizzling kiss that left her weak-kneed and shaky and breathless.

When his lips finally eased off hers, she sagged against him, boneless, her hard-fought well-honed resolve in tatters.

'Never thought I'd get a chance to do that again.'

He kissed the soft skin behind her ear, a gentle, barely there brush of his lips that made her sway as she whimpered, a soft, needy sound betraying her solid stance of not falling further for him.

When he raised his head, his glittering, passion-filled gaze implored her to acknowledge the heat between them.

'I got the message loud and clear, you don't want this, but it doesn't make it any easier to resist you.'

She couldn't think, couldn't breathe, her senses filled with his closeness, his heat, the thought she was irresistible to him as heady as his touch.

She gasped as he slid his fingers under the dress's slit, trailing a lazy fingertip along her thigh upwards.

It would be so easy to give in, so easy to succumb. She knew what would happen, remembered in excruciatingly erotic detail what would follow if she forgot her reservations for one night, if she just let go.

Her skin prickled, her body leaning towards him in yearning, desperate for his touch.

So easy to lose herself in the moment...

'I've tried, Charli, damn I've tried. But I want you. And I'm leaving. And this all got screwed up.'

He held her at arm's length, his stormy gaze reflecting the torture and confusion in hers.

She wanted him too, but for more than just a hot

goodbye, a quickie for old times' sake. She wanted so much more than that and he couldn't give it to her.

Yet standing here, torn between giving in and fleeing, she wavered between following her head—telling her to run as fast as she could—and giving in to her heart, craving one last momentous, stupendous night with him before he left.

From the first moment he'd opened his hotel-room door wearing a towel and a wicked smile she'd been drawn to him, tempted beyond belief. And in the past few minutes, when all it had taken was one scintillating kiss to undermine her resolve of the past week, she knew that for all her self-talk and self-control he still had the power to break her heart in a second.

That was what settled her dilemma. Her head was right and her heart couldn't stand breaking any more than it already was.

'Tonight's important to Hector. Let's go.'

The fire in his eyes faded and he released her, a cold shiver pebbling her skin with goose bumps at the sudden loss of his heat.

'Always on the job, Charli?'

'Always,' she said, grabbing her evening bag and pre-ceding him out of the door so he couldn't see her stoic expression crumple.

'Pop's in his element.' Charli followed Luca's subtle head jerk towards the dance floor. 'Who knew the old guy could break a move or two?'

She smiled and his world tilted slightly off kilter. He had the same gut reaction every time he caught a glimpse of one of her rare smiles these days, all too rare the past week. She'd been the epitome of the perfect tour manager: driven, dedicated, a dervish. He respected her work ethic but it had been a front, a very convenient front she'd hidden behind to keep him from getting too close.

He should know, he'd done the same, maintaining a polite indifference until he thought he'd go nuts.

Damn, her rejection had stung, more than he could've thought possible and that in itself was a major clue to how seriously out of his depth he was.

He didn't do emotions for a reason and this was it, this convoluted, befuddled confusion that scrambled his brains and made him crave something he couldn't have until it was all he could think about.

He knew it was pointless, wanting Charli this badly, for she'd pushed him away in no uncertain terms. And the kicker, it made *sense*. Why continue their fling, for that was all it could ever be, when he was out of here soon?

Oh, yeah, it made perfect sense, them not rekindling the fire between them, but that didn't make accepting it any easier.

He'd hated catching her in an unguarded moment, glimpsing the chariness mingled with hurt in her eyes, her wounded expression making him shrivel a little more inside.

She'd never recovered from the way he'd treated her after they'd had sex in Bendigo and, no matter how many times he rehashed it in his head, he knew he couldn't have done it differently.

Then too he'd been stung by her rejection and he'd reacted badly, throwing out that callous comment. He didn't take kindly to rejection—yet another thing to thank dear old Dad for—and it messed with his head.

Now he only had two days left before he flew back to London and, while he should be grateful to leave all this angst behind, he couldn't stop this all-consuming, all-driving need to hold her in his arms one last time.

A crazy, futile wish he had no intention of acting on yet it was there all the same, omnipresent, overwhelming, driving him nuts.

He hadn't intended on laying a hand on her earlier but when she'd opened the door and he'd taken one look at her in that sexy gold dress he'd lost it. Completely.

Though it hadn't been all bad. She'd responded to his kiss, had kissed him back with the same unbridled passion they'd had in Bendigo and it gave him hope that maybe, just maybe, he wasn't so crazy in still wanting her, that despite her calculated indifference she still wanted him too.

'Hector loves the Arias. Loves it when Landry's recording artists win gongs, loves the vibe, loves—'

'The girls?'

He raised an eyebrow as Pop left the dance floor with two young girls a quarter his age on each arm.

'Looks like he's not the only one.'

She pointed to Storm, who'd just been inducted into the rock-and-roll hall of fame, and was celebrating with a curvy blonde on each arm.

'Why aren't you out there partying?'

'Because I'm right where I want to be.'

He risked taking her hand, not surprised when she slid it out from his on the pretext of having a sip of her Pinot Noir.

He shouldn't have kissed her earlier, shouldn't have pushed his luck but no way in hell was he sorry for it.

'So you're flying out after the concert tomorrow night?'

She was trying to make small-talk, to prevent the focus from potentially getting onto shaky ground—namely them—but if he didn't give this one last shot now he'd never know.

'Yeah, some big shindig in London the next evening I need to attend.'

'Straight back into the fray for you, then?'

'Yeah, I guess.'

She wasn't judging him but he heard the resignation in her voice, wondered why the thought of him leaving was hitting her this hard, especially when she hadn't wanted a bar of him over the past week.

They'd flirted, they'd connected, they'd had one afternoon of monumental sex and that was it. Why was she so maudlin at the thought of him leaving?

Unless...

No. No way. Surely she wasn't emotionally invested?

Was *that* why she'd backed off? To stop from getting in deeper?

Man, he was such an idiot. Why hadn't he seen it sooner? If anyone should know about emotional avoidance, he should. It had been a major reason he'd run all those years ago, couldn't bear getting attached to the only family he had left for fear Pop would eventually reject him too.

Pop's overtures to close the gap between them back then had been stilted at best and if his grandfather hadn't been able to love him unreservedly as a kid, what chance would he have had later?

Much easier to cut and run and not risk further problems and, in a way, their cool relationship over the years vindicated the choice he'd made. Pop and he weren't close and, while it saddened him at times, it was better this way.

Was that what Charli had done, push him away before things got complicated?

'Can I ask you something?' He slipped her hand into his, intertwining fingers and holding tight when she tried to escape again.

'Depends.'

He hated the caution in her eyes, the fact he'd put it there.

'If I wasn't leaving tomorrow night, would things be different?'

She ducked her head behind her shiny blonde hair hanging in a sleek curtain around her face, but not before he'd seen her guilty flash-away glance.

'Would you—?'

He cut off the rest of what he'd been about to ask as Hector leaned over their chairs and slapped him on the back.

'Glad to see my employees getting in a little bonding time.' He pointed at their joined hands and grinned. 'You two make a great team.'

A tiny frown creased Charli's brow as she subtly tried to yank her hand free. He held on tighter.

'You run a tight ship, Pop. Stands to reason your employees are so friendly.'

Hector guffawed and slapped him on the back. 'That's my boy. Now, you kids enjoy yourselves. I'm off to party.'

They watched him cut a swathe through the crowd, back-slapping cronies and wooing women.

'He's something else,' he muttered, shaking his head in admiration. 'And he's right, you know.'

'About?'

He squeezed her hand. 'We do make a great team.'

She stiffened, shook her head slightly. 'We're nothing alike.'

'Aren't we?'

He lifted her hand to his mouth, placed a soft kiss on the back of it, savouring the slight tremble that made him hold on tighter.

'We both play our cards close to our chest. We both see the world for what it is, with no illusions.'

He touched her cheek, a fleeting brush of fingertips against her skin, trying to convey what he was feeling—whatever that confusing jumble of emotions was—with a simple touch.

'We're both wary of getting emotionally involved.'

There, he'd thrown it out there, what he believed to be the reason why she'd backed off the past week.

Her eyes widened, making him wish he could drown in all that beguiling green.

'That's it, isn't it? The reason you've backed away?'

She didn't have to speak. He saw the answer in her quick look-away glance, in the worrying of her bottom lip, before she carefully eradicated all emotion from her face, fixing her deliberately blank gaze at some spot over his left shoulder.

'Charli?'

He touched her knee when he wanted to bundle her into his arms and hold her tight until her aloofness melted and he saw the real woman underneath, the woman with warmth and sparks and fire.

'Look at me.'

She wrenched her gaze back to his, the shimmer of fear all the confirmation he needed he'd nailed it.

Tilting her chin up, she stared him down, defiant.

'Doesn't change a thing.'

Damn it, she was right. He was still leaving in two days; she was scared of letting him in.

But she cared about him. She'd virtually admitted it with her muttered, *'Doesn't change a thing.'*

Though she was wrong. It changed everything.

Taking hold of both her hands, he wouldn't let go when she tugged.

'This wasn't a fling for me.'

'No, it was a one-afternoon stand.'

Her cool tone made a mockery of what they'd shared and he was damned if he'd tolerate that.

'Bull. Disregarding the sex, which was phenomenal, we've connected this last fortnight. And you know I don't connect with people. Ever.'

He'd been terrified of emotionally connecting with her yet he'd gone ahead and done it anyway and that spoke volumes about how far gone he was. He was under her spell, totally, utterly bewitched, and something that had once scared him to death—connecting with another person—wasn't so intimidating any more.

Her tongue darted out to moisten her bottom lip and he could've sworn her hands trembled, her almost-imperceptible nod urging him to go for broke.

'You don't owe me anything but I think you owe yourself the truth. I've opened up to you and that's taken some guts on my part. If you don't admit the truth to yourself now, you never will.'

When she lifted her eyes to his, the shimmer of tears slugged him hard.

'Fine, I care, damn it. Happy?'

'Are *you*?'

Releasing a hand, he tipped her chin up, leaving her no option but to meet his steady gaze.

Silence stretched between them and he'd almost given up hope when she finally shook her head and murmured, 'No.'

Knowing he was racing against the clock, he closed

the distance between them and brushed a soft kiss against her trembling lips.

'So what are we going to do about it?'

CHAPTER TWELVE

TWENTY-FOUR hours later, Charli was even more drained if that were possible.

'You two aren't bad for a couple of control freaks.'

She tried not to cringe as Storm draped an arm across her shoulder, the other on Luca's, who looked as if he'd deck the drunken rock star given half a chance.

'If you're thanking us for making your comeback tour the best ever, you're welcome,' Charli said, her dry response going over Storm's alcohol-hazed head but garnering a wry grin from Luca.

'Time for you two to let loose.' Storm raised his arms in a victory salute, releasing them from his clutches. 'I'm the best. The concert rocked. Melbourne loved me.'

Slapping them on the backs for good measure, he slurred, 'My work is done. Party on.'

As Storm stumbled away Luca said, 'That's one part of Melbourne I definitely won't miss.'

She watched Storm lurch through the band, bumping heads with the lead guitarist, and winced.

'I thought you had a new-found respect for our resident rock star after the country tour.'

'It vanished when he ripped off those leather chaps he wore tonight and threw them into the crowd.' Luca shuddered. 'Man, who knows where those chaps have been?'

She laughed, for what felt like the first time in ages and it felt good, really good, after the way she'd been buttoned up this past week, repressing her natural responses to Luca for fear of releasing her fragile grip on her resistance to him.

She couldn't believe he'd guessed the truth last night. No one had ever seen the real her yet in less than two weeks he'd managed to undermine her, unhinge her and understand her.

And what he'd said resonated. She wasn't happy, had been downright miserable the past week, holding back for fear of falling deeper for him when in reality nothing she could do or say would stave off the inevitable.

Luca was the type of guy you fell for.

And just for one night, she was through being logical and careful. She wanted to make this night count.

'You're enjoying the after-party?'

He shrugged and she stifled a sigh as the simple action pulled his black silk shirt taut across his chest. 'I'd rather be elsewhere for my last eight hours in Melbourne.'

She swallowed to ease the tightness in her throat. He could've meant anything by that comment. Maybe he had loads of packing to do. Maybe he had to tie up last-minute handover notes for the incoming finance manager. Maybe he just wanted to get away from the noise and excitement of Storm's final comeback concert and chill out before he boarded a plane.

But as she snuck a glimpse at him and saw the same soul-deep longing flash across his face for an instant before it was gone, she knew exactly how he'd like to spend his last eight hours in this city.

Was he feeling the same desperation, the same confusion, the same yearning? Desperate to make their last eight hours together count, confused that this would only make saying goodbye harder, yearning for one, last, cataclysmic night together to savour later when they'd parted for good?

Torn between doing the sensible thing, the right thing and the all-out crazy thing, she clenched and unclenched her fingers several times, shaking them out, belatedly realising the incessant tingling had more to do with his proximity than any pins and needles.

She should say her goodbyes and walk away now.

But as she glanced up and caught a flicker of desolation in his unwavering gaze, she knew she couldn't walk away. Not like this.

Drawing in a shaky breath, she went for broke.

'Where would you like to spend your last hours in Melbourne?'

His eyes darkened as he surreptitiously threaded his fingers through hers and tugged her closer.

'You know.'

Yeah, she knew and ever since she'd begged off him taking her home from the Arias last night citing babysitting Storm duties, all day when they'd been manic ensuring the concert tonight went off without a hitch, and over the past few hours when Storm had belted out hit after hit to an adoring Melbourne crowd, she'd tried to stay focused on her job and not on the knowledge that was driving her mad.

That despite the self-defeating ramifications, she had to say a proper goodbye to Luca Petrelli.

'That was out of line, Charli, forget it—'

He released her hand and took a step back, steeling his expression into one of cool resignation but not before she'd seen the fleeting anguish they wouldn't have a chance at a proper goodbye.

Still no closer to knowing if she was doing the right thing and with her heart thundering in her ears, she took a deep breath, looked him straight in the eye and said, 'Come on. Let's make your last few hours in Melbourne count.'

'You know this is a really bad idea, right?'

In response Luca backed her up against her front door, clasped her wrists, brought them overhead and plundered her mouth in a devastating kiss that left her weak-kneed when he eventually came up for air.

'Very bad idea,' he murmured, nuzzling her neck, nipping the tender skin above her collarbone, licking a trail along her cleavage until she moaned.

'We've spent a week trying to avoid this.'

She gasped as he slid an arm around her waist and angled her pelvis snugly into his, where she found excellent evidence to stop talking and make the most of their time together.

'A wasted week,' he said, pinning her wrists to the door with one hand and using the other to bring her flush against him, playing her like a double bass. A double bass in desperate need of some fine-tuning.

'We really going to do this?' she asked.

He stopped kissing her bare shoulder and released his grip on her wrists, waiting 'til her arms fell to her sides before locking his around her.

'Only if you want to.'

He was giving her an out; after all their dancing around each other and holding back, with desire pounding through their bodies and heat shimmering between them, he was still giving her the option to stop, giving her total control and in that moment she knew what it felt like to be truly empowered.

Heady stuff, for a girl tossed on the streets—powerless—and a woman who spent her life trying to regain power by staying on top of her job, staying in control all the time.

Sliding her hands around to his butt, she tugged him towards her. 'Come inside and I'll show you what I want.'

His jubilant curse echoed what they were about to do as they fumbled the lock and fell through the door in haste.

'We're making a habit of that,' she said, suddenly nervous when he kicked the door shut and advanced on her.

'Happens when two people can't get enough of each other.'

He took a step towards her and a flood of need drenched her, quelling her nerves and making her want him more than ever.

She was through prevaricating. She wanted this, wanted him and no way in hell would she back down now.

'You know that, right? I can't get enough of you?'

Another step and she nodded, holding her breath as his potent gaze started at the top of her shoulders where spaghetti straps held up her little black dress and slowly worked its way down, lingering on her breasts until her nipples pebbled, skimming her waist, focusing on her pelvis until she squirmed, wet and waiting.

'Luca, please…' Her plea came out a whimper as he took another step closer, within touching distance now, the crackle of electricity between them as real and potent as the first time.

'I intend to please you.'

With his hands hanging loosely by his sides, his clenched fists the only sign the effort not to touch her was killing him, he locked gazes with her, the depth of his need notching up her own to boiling point.

'All night long.'

She gasped as he ducked his head, slanting a soft kiss across her lips, working his way towards her ear where he proceeded to tell her exactly what he planned on doing.

In exquisite, excruciating, erotic detail.

By the time he'd finished she was swaying towards him, on the verge of an orgasm, desperate to be pushed over the edge.

'Think you can handle that?'

In response she flung herself against him, knocking over a lamp and not giving a damn.

Their mouths clashed in an explosion of mutual need, his hands clasping her to him as she ground against him once, twice and fell apart, screaming his name.

It wasn't enough. She wanted more. She wanted it all.

'Not a bad prelude. You ready for the encore?'

Blown away by the enormity of all this, she held up a finger. 'Give me a minute.'

He snagged her hand as she backed towards her bedroom, hoping it wouldn't take too long to create a private party for two. Now she'd finally thrown her reservations away, she wanted to make tonight memorable, a night neither of them would ever forget, a night to remember in the weeks to come when she slowly put her broken heart back together.

'Make it thirty seconds and you've got a deal.'

He tugged her in for a sizzling kiss that left her hoping she could light the candles and oil burner in fifteen.

'Clock's ticking,' he murmured, his hand sliding over her butt as she eased out of his grasp.

'Patience, virtue, remember?'

He tapped his watch. 'Twenty seconds and counting.'

She rushed into the bedroom and scurried around, lighting tea candles and spritzing the air with ylang-ylang, an essential oil she loved. Glancing around the room, she experienced a moment of panic. Was she really doing this? Inviting him into her bedroom, setting the scene for seduction, giving herself to him one last time?

The flames from the tea lights twinkled, winking at her, as if they were in on the plan right from the very start.

But she hadn't planned this. She liked candles, liked essential oils, and always wound down at the end of a busy day by lighting tea lights, firing up the oil burner, plugging her iPod on and lying on the bed with her eyes closed, letting the stress of the day dissipate.

Sadly, her usual de-stressors weren't working now. Dragging in deep breaths, she pressed a hand to her belly, willing the tumbling to subside.

In a second she'd open the door and let Luca into her heart for the very last time.

Her hand drifted upwards to her chest, rubbing away the ache that morphed and spread at the thought of saying goodbye. The thing was, regardless if she made love to him or not, this horrible ache would still be there. It would take time, a long time, before she recovered from loving and losing Luca. Surely having an incredible memory of their parting would help ease the pain?

She closed her eyes and inhaled, the sweet scent teasing her senses and she emptied her mind, allowing calm to flow through her.

She could do this. Bid Luca a proper farewell, one that would sustain her in the lonely nights ahead when she smelled this fragrance and was catapulted back to this night.

Filled with a new resolve, she opened her eyes and eased down the zip on her black sheath, thankful she'd worn her best lingerie, needing all the confidence she could get to show Luca how much he meant to her one last time.

As if thinking about him conjured him, he knocked once on the door.

'Colour me impatient but I'm not waiting out here one more damn second.'

'Come in,' she called out, stepping out of her sheath as he stepped into the bedroom, his gaze zeroing in on her like a heat-seeking missile.

She shivered in anticipation as his burning eyes stripped her of the ebony lace sheer teddy, her choice in lingerie vindicated by the speed in which he crossed her bedroom and hauled her into his arms.

'Utterly divine.'

She bit back a moan as he nuzzled her neck. 'It's ylang-ylang. And some of the candles are scented too—'

'I'm not talking about the candles and you know it.'

He lifted his head and when his heavy-lidded gaze met !.ers, she stopped breathing. For in that instant she could've sworn he cared as much as she did.

Her heart wobbled with the impact. Had Luca fallen for her? Was his reluctance over the past week a product of the same fear she'd secretly harboured? A fear of getting too close, a fear of falling too far?

She stared into all that beautiful blue, lost in his eyes, drowning in a pool of longing so deep she'd happily never surface.

If he felt half of what she did, this parting would be more bittersweet than she had possibly imagined.

'Leaving you is going to be the hardest thing—'

She kissed away the rest of his words, not wanting to waste a moment talking. She wanted a night to remember, a night filled with precious memories.

For now she wanted to show him how she felt.

She deepened the kiss, teasing his tongue, running hers along his bottom lip, sucking it into her mouth until he groaned.

Her hands wrenched his shirt free from his trousers, her fingertips hitting pay dirt when they skated across the warm skin at the base of his spine.

He moaned into her mouth as her fingers skimmed his waist, light as a feather, coming to rest over his belt buckle.

With their mouths fused and their tongues dancing, she slid the leather strap of his belt out of its loophole, her fingers trembling as she toyed with the buckle.

He stilled her hand and broke the kiss, resting his forehead against hers as their uneven breaths mingled.

'Charli, I wish—'

She placed her fingers against his lips.

'Shh…later.'

Her fingertips traced his lips, enjoyed the slight quiver of his bottom lip when her nail scraped it.

'Much later.'

In response, he ripped the teddy off her, the scraps

of lace a lost remnant in their passion as he backed her onto the bed and eased her down.

His hands lingered at her ankles, stroked upwards, caressing the inside of her thighs until she quivered. He splayed her, opening her to him as her body thrummed with tension, burning beneath the hunger in his ravenous gaze.

He knelt before her, worshipping, as his hands slid under her hips and lifted her pelvis. He lowered his head so slowly she cramped with need, her muscles taut, desperate to unravel at the first flick of his tongue.

She arched into his mouth, frantic for the release only he could give her, her erotic memories of how many times he'd done this in Bendigo mingling with the present and intensifying the pleasure until she thought she'd explode.

Propping up on her elbows, she watched him, their gazes locked as he finally, exquisitely, touched his mouth to her and with the first circle of his tongue on her she came undone, surging up to thread her fingers through his hair, bucking against his mouth as he continued to pleasure her long after the first shudders had subsided.

With her body boneless with pleasure after she'd orgasmed twice, she shimmied up the bed and crooked a finger at him.

He didn't have to be asked twice, lunging at her, their frantic hands making quick work of his clothes.

In moments they were skin to skin, slick and wanting, their lips fused as he sank onto the bed, protected, and pulled her onto his lap.

She straddled him and slid down slowly, prolonging the exquisite agony until she enveloped him and he groaned, long and loud.

She needed him now. She wanted him now. She loved him now…

Loved? She *loved* him?

With the desperate clamouring of their bodies as he thrust up and she slid down repeatedly, their tension building and spiralling, all she could focus on was the fact she'd just realised she hadn't just fallen for this amazing man, she loved him.

As he thrust up once more, harder and deeper, and she tipped over the edge and screamed out his name, she slumped into his arms, wishing they had a future yet knowing she'd given up on wishes a long time ago.

When the last candle burned low Luca brushed a soft kiss across Charli's forehead and slid out of bed.

He'd spent the last half-hour watching her: the gentle rise and fall of the sheet draped over her breasts, the tiny tilt of her lips at the corners, the soft skin of her eyelids fluttering as she dreamed.

If what they'd done over the past five hours was any indication, they'd be pleasant dreams indeed.

She blew his mind in so many ways he could barely count them yet when she woke he wouldn't be here. He couldn't be. He'd said his goodbyes, putting his words into actions, demonstrating repeatedly all night how special she was, how she made him feel.

Like a better man, a man who could conquer the world.

And that alone was enough to send him running to catch his flight.

He relied on no one, and knowing Charli held that much power over him seriously screwed with his head.

To make matters worse he'd seen the moment of truth,

that one fantastical moment when she'd been straddling him the first time, her skin sweat-slicked and glistening, her hair tumbling like spun gold around her shoulders, her eyes pinned on his...with love in their depths.

He now knew why she'd been so scared the past week. She hadn't been afraid of becoming emotionally invested, she was already there, and tonight had tipped her over the edge.

She couldn't love him because he couldn't love her in return. Simply, he didn't know how.

After their chat at the Arias last night he'd contemplated returning to Melbourne regularly, getting to know Pop better, maybe trialling a long-distance relationship with Charli.

But after seeing the depth of her feelings tonight, that was out of the question. The further this developed, the longer this continued, the greater her heartbreak and no way in hell would he put her through that.

He knew what it felt like having your heart ripped out of your chest and trampled on—Rad had seen to that—no way in hell would he put a woman as special as Charli, a woman he cared about, through that.

No, it was better this way. They'd said all that needed to be said; with every whispered endearment, with every murmured plea, they'd said their goodbyes.

Best to walk away now.

While he still could.

CHAPTER THIRTEEN

CHARLI knew Luca had gone the moment her eyes fluttered open to the pale gold dawn filtering through the wooden slats.

She lay in bed, shallow breathing, staring at the ceiling and refusing to cry, the ache in her chest spreading outwards, filling her with a gut-wrenching pain that had her rolling over onto her side and clutching her middle.

She'd known this was how she'd feel when he left: gutted. Empty. Grief-stricken.

But she'd gone ahead last night anyway and now wasn't the time for regrets or self-flagellation. She had to get on with her life, starting with heading into the office and instigating the first steps to get Storm Varth to sign on with Landry Records for his much-anticipated new release.

Running on false determination, she hauled herself out of bed, slipped into a robe and padded into the bathroom.

Logically she shouldn't be this upset. She knew he was leaving, was probably best this way with no prolonged teary farewell. But glancing around the bathroom, all evidence of his presence wiped clean, something deep inside her finally broke.

Not for what they'd done, but for what he couldn't do.

Luca couldn't get emotionally involved.

He didn't know how but with every touch, every caress, last night, she'd hoped he would.

And while her heart cracked piece by piece, she didn't hold him responsible. When you'd been rejected growing up it became second nature not to trust. She knew that firsthand. So while she didn't blame him for not knowing how to love, she did blame him for not wanting to try.

She loved the most amazing, charming, gregarious, gorgeous man on the planet.

And he didn't love her back.

As the enormity of the situation sank in, the protective wall around her heavily guarded heart cracked and crumbled, taking the last of her stoic bravery with it as she slumped onto the edge of the bathtub and bawled.

She had no idea how long she sat there, choking sobs racking her body until she ached all over. For someone who rarely cried, it felt as if a decade's worth of tears spilled out for all she'd lost.

When her mum had first kicked her out, she'd been too shocked to cry, had deliberately focused on the numbness pervading her heart so she could block out the terrifying reality of surviving on the streets. And over the years she'd realised Sharon wasn't worth her tears.

Luca, on the other hand, had opened a floodgate by leaving and she cried until she had nothing left, clutching her middle as she stood and avoided looking in the mirror.

She should jump in the shower, get dressed and head to work, the one unwavering comfort in her life. Instead, she shuffled into the bedroom, took one look at the bed and fell into it, curling up into a foetal position, wishing she could stem the awful sadness creeping through her, a thief stealthily robbing her of every happy moment she'd spent with Luca.

Rolling over, she buried her face in a pillow, *his* pillow, his familiar crisp lime and sexy male scent a momentary comfort. Until she realised she'd never get to bury her nose in the crook of his neck and smell it again.

All those wasted nights... Fury replaced her sorrow and she sat bolt upright, clutching his pillow to her with one hand and thumping hers with the other.

She'd been so hell-bent on safeguarding her heart, so focused on burying the hurt after his fling comment, she'd lost sight of reality. A reality she now couldn't ignore: she loved him, had probably loved him when she'd slept with him the first time.

Why else would his throwaway comment have hurt so much? Why else would she have spent an entire week deliberately pushing him away unless she was absolutely terrified of falling any deeper?

Her head dropped and she clutched his pillow tighter, wishing she had her time over again. She'd wasted seven long nights to make the most of every second with a guy she'd never forget.

She'd been so sure of herself, so steady in her resolve to guard her heart, deluding herself into believing she could handle one last night and then concentrate on forgetting.

Cursing her stupidity and vulnerability, she flung the pillow away and knuckled her eyes, pressing to stem a new influx of tears.

It didn't work and as she covered her face with her hands she knew it would take a lifetime to recover from loving Luca.

***

Luca strode the airport corridors like a man possessed, willing his plane to land so it could take off again, taking him as far from this godforsaken city as possible.

The last time he'd felt this rattled, this hollow, had been after his father's funeral when his so-called family had booted him out.

Oh, it was fine for them to grieve and console each other and show solidarity, but an eighteen-year-old kid who needed that family, their acknowledgement more than ever? They'd turned their collective backs on him.

He'd tried to ignore the bitterness growing up, tried to be a man as he watched his mum pine away for a bastard who didn't give a rat's about anyone but himself.

He'd learned to never carry emotional baggage, to ignore the constant worry that whatever he did it wouldn't be good enough in the end. That little life lesson had been driven in hard every time his father turned away and pretended he didn't exist.

Not risking emotional ties was definitely for the best. It had served him well enough for years: working to raise money for the charities but not getting too involved, dating but never seeing the same woman beyond a few weeks, staying in touch with Hector but never moving beyond polite necessities.

Yet in the face of the warm, vibrant woman he'd left sleeping in bed two hours ago, why did his life suddenly seem so empty?

He stopped short, the reality hitting him, and he muttered an apology as a woman slammed into him from behind. Resettling her, and ignoring the moment her frown blossomed into a flirtatious smile, he headed for the nearest bar and downed a whisky straight.

When the barman asked if he'd like another, he

shook his head, pointed at his empty glass and muttered, 'Medicinal purposes.'

The barman's dubious expression said he'd heard that one many times before and, leaving a generous tip, Luca resumed his pacing.

Heading back to London to his well-ordered, clinical life had seemed the best option. Until he'd realised why the life he'd carefully cultivated suddenly seemed cold and dull and lifeless.

He *felt* something for Charli.

Something that went beyond caring.

Something he couldn't identify but could well be bordering on...*love*?

But how could it be, when he couldn't recognise what he was feeling? Was this helpless, out-of-control, panicky feeling love? And if so, what the hell was he going to do about it?

He could spend the next twenty-four hours on a plane stewing over this or he could take a risk on reaching out to someone.

Cursing under his breath, he fished his mobile out of his pocket and hit Pop on speed dial.

'Luca, my boy, how are you?'

'I stuffed up.'

To his credit Pop didn't jump to conclusions or rant or interrogate. He paused, giving him time to continue.

'With Charli.'

As if he needed clarification.

'What happened?'

'I've made a mess of things.'

Inhaling, he pinched the bridge of his nose before blurting the truth.

'I think I'm in love with her.'

'So what's the problem?'

He heard the cynicism in Pop's voice and it increased the tightness gripping his chest. This was a mistake, ringing a man he'd deliberately kept at arm's length over the years, hoping for advice.

But he was desperate and anything Pop could offer him in the way of counsel would be better than going out of his mind during the long-haul flight.

'I don't know what love is.'

He hated how pitiful he sounded, how utterly clueless when he'd handled millions the world over.

If Pop didn't have the answers he was royally stuffed.

'Of course you do! You lived with it every day.'

He stiffened, clutching the phone so tight he thought it'd snap. He'd never heard Hector raise his voice and the fact he was doing it now stung.

'Never mind—'

'Your mother was a determined, proud woman who foolishly loved my pompous-ass son, but she loved you too.'

Pop cursed and Luca stared at the phone, stunned. 'Did you know the only reason she accepted money for your schooling was because I pulled a swifty? I paid your entire high-school tuition up front and told her if she didn't let you go, the school would just spend it on even more stuff for the already over-privileged kids who went there rather than her son and she finally relented.'

'I never knew,' he said, adding guilt to his jumble of emotions. All the times he'd blamed his mum for not loving him enough…she hadn't just been after Rad's money. If she had, she would've leapt at Pop's offer to pay for his education, which cost several hundred thousand. That meant she had him because she wanted to and in going her own way to provide for both of them she'd proven her love time and time again.

'Well now you do. So don't go using your past as an excuse to stuff up your future.'

Luca had no idea what he'd expected to hear from Pop but, whatever it was, this wasn't it. He'd expected a friendly ear, some sympathy, not this blunt lecture.

That'd teach him for reaching out.

'My flight's about to board. Got to go.'

'What about Charli?'

An image of her sleeping peacefully before he ran out on her stuck in his mind on rewind, cleaving a giant hole in his heart.

'I'll ring her.'

Pop's judgemental silence didn't bode well and before he could launch into another broadside, Luca said, 'See you.'

He didn't wait for a response, ending the call with a stab at the phone, his hand shaking as he slid the phone back into his pocket.

Nothing was going right. First he'd stuffed up with Charli and by the sounds of that phone call he'd done the same with Pop.

This was what letting emotion into his life did: caused chaos and confusion.

So what the hell was he going to do to make things right?

Lucky the flight to London was a long one. He had a lot of thinking to do.

After stumbling around in a daze for an hour, Charli finally snapped out of her funk. Having the fastest shower on record, she threw on her favourite business suit, a deep crimson knee-skimming skirt and long jacket, guaranteed to give her a confidence boost. She felt so crappy, she needed it.

Dreading heading to work—and seeing reminders of Luca everywhere—for the first time ever, she opened the front door as the phone rang. She waited, holding her breath, hoping it was Luca while chastising herself for being a coward and not picking up.

The moment his voice boomed from the answering machine, her knees shook and she gripped the door.

'Hey, Charli, it's me. Sorry for being a monumental jerk. If you're there, pick up.'

She strode back to the phone, her hand hovering over it, before falling to her side.

If she answered she'd probably fall apart and make a fool of herself or, worse, beg him to stay. They'd said their goodbyes, in actions if not words. What was the point now?

'Guess you're screening. Don't blame you after I ran out of there without saying a proper goodbye. Anyway, I'd really like to talk.'

Her breath caught at his sincerity and she waited, hoping for some small sign he cared as much as she did.

'Okay, then, take care of yourself.'

He rang off, the silence exacerbating the emptiness in her heart.

He wanted to talk. Talk about what? Why he liked her and they'd connected and he'd had a good time but adios and thanks for the memories? No, the time for talking was long past. She loved him, and if he hadn't understood that after last night he never would.

Though was she being too harsh? Guys could never

read the signs and someone as emotionally closed off as Luca would find it more difficult than most. Besides, what if he did know? It wouldn't change a thing.

She supposed she'd have to talk to him eventually but for now she had to immerse herself in work, the one thing guaranteed to take her mind off her bleeding heart.

If only it could staunch the agony too.

Luca had soul-searched over the past few days.

While he'd been in London physically, finalising some details on financing for a major kids' cancer charity, emotionally he'd been back in Melbourne, wondering what Charli was doing, wondering if she was okay, wondering if she'd give him another chance when he returned.

He'd tried calling her again with limited success before he'd figured out what he had to say couldn't be done over the phone. What did he think, that she'd pick up and he'd blurt 'I love you'? Yeah, as if she'd believe that after the way he'd treated her.

No, what he had to say had to be done face to face and he'd mentally rehearsed his spiel countless times on the long flight from London to Melbourne.

So he'd had to wait and while he'd like nothing better than to rush over and see her right this very minute, he first had something else to take care of, for he knew if he didn't get a handle on his past he might make a mess of his future.

He'd been seriously ticked off with the way Hector had chastised him for being a fool when he'd called out of desperation from the airport, until he'd mulled it at length and realised something. Pop's no-nonsense straight-talking was exactly the way a father would treat his son—brusque, frank, no mincing words—and his initial resentment had faded, leaving him empty.

He'd dealt with the emptiness over the years, had filled it with work and raising money and giving until he felt good, but now it simply wasn't enough. And if he was willing to let Charli into his life, maybe it was time to show Pop the same courtesy?

Striding up to the imposing glossy black double doors of Pop's mansion, he remembered the first time he'd skipped up this path, holding on to his mum's hand, filled with curiosity and excitement.

He'd heard so many stories of the Landrys, Australia's most famous music family. His mum had filled his head with images of a castle, with sparkling lights and cascading fountains and shiny floors. He'd expected to be cherished in this castle. He couldn't have been more wrong.

His mum never made the mistake of bringing him here again after that first time, when his father had been summoned by the butler, taken one look at him and slammed the door in their faces.

She'd tried other ways to introduce them, each more cringe-worthy and embarrassing than the last until he'd hit his early teens and threatened to move out if she tried another 'meet Rad and bond' stunt.

He'd learned to pretend it didn't matter, that not having a dad at Father's Day breakfast at school, parents and kids' footy games and his graduation wasn't a big deal, but it did, and he never forgave Rad for not caring about him when he'd done nothing wrong, nothing other than being born.

Letting himself in with a key Hector had pressed on him years earlier and he'd never used, he headed for the conservatory where Pop would be having his nightly

Shiraz. While he'd spent his life cultivating a footloose lifestyle, from what he'd seen over the past few weeks Pop favoured predictability.

He paused in the doorway, watching Pop puff on a Cuban cigar, a full glass of Shiraz at his right hand, tapping the arm rest of his recliner as he listened to his favourite Glen Miller remix. The big band crescendoed and Pop conducted with his cigar, lost in an era of brass and woodwind.

Reluctant to interrupt his relaxation but needing to get this over with so he could visit Charli, he stepped into the glass-enclosed room.

'You still smoking those cancer sticks?'

Pop glanced up, the initial caution in his eyes giving way to a grin as welcoming as it was the first time they'd met.

'If they don't kill me, this will.' He raised the Shiraz in a silent toast. 'But damn, I'll go happy.'

Considering he'd pushed this man away his entire life, he didn't have the right to lecture so settled for silence as he took a seat opposite.

'Glad you finally used the key.'

He waited for an 'about time' but Pop merely puffed on his cigar.

'Anything happen while I was away?'

'You mean apart from me keeping an eye on Charli?'

It took all his will power not to leap out of the chair at the mention of her name.

'How is she?'

'Fine. For a woman so besotted by you she can't concentrate on work.'

Pop matched his belligerent glare. 'She's been

mooning around the office the last few days. No surprises why.'

'She probably wants to throttle me in person.'

The scepticism in Pop's eyes faded, replaced by the genuine fondness he'd craved growing up.

'She loves you, son. Don't mess it up this time.'

Son... That one small word unravelled him, made him feel about ten years old and just as needy of approval and love.

But all he could focus on now was the fact Pop said Charli loved him. He thought she loved him...though they'd never really made any declarations...and after the way he'd run out on her...

'I'm heading over there as soon as we're done.'

Pop gulped half his Shiraz before placing the glass on the side table with a sigh.

'What's so important you visited me first?'

'I need to talk about Rad.'

Luca avoided looking over Pop's right shoulder, at the grand piano covered in family pictures. He could never stomach seeing his father's smug face, the arrogance he wore like a designer suit.

'Your father wanted to bridge the gap between you, he just never knew how.'

Luca fought to keep his top lip from curling into a snarl.

'When was that? After he'd ignored me the first five years? Or the next ten?'

He leapt from his chair and started pacing. 'He never recognised I was his son. Mum tried, you tried. So there's nothing you can say that'll convince me he was anything but a callous bastard.'

Pop stubbed out his cigar and rose to his feet, reaching out a hand he ignored.

'Then why are you here?'

'Because I want to know why, damn it! I was hoping you might have some answers so I—'

'Go on, son.'

Luca stopped dead and gripped the back of the nearest chair. 'So I don't end up like him, an emotional cripple.'

'You already love Charli so you're capable of feeling a lot more than Rad ever did,' Hector said, his tone weary. 'And I should know.'

Sinking into the nearest chair, Luca dropped his head into his hands.

'I don't understand.'

With a heavy sigh, Pop pulled up a chair nearby. 'This is partially my fault.'

He raised his head. 'How can this remotely be your fault?'

Pop paled, his sombre expression sending a shiver of dread through Luca.

'Rad couldn't be a father to you because he didn't know how. He'd never had a good example to begin with.'

Confused, Luca shook his head. 'But you've always been there—'

'For you.'

Pop's hand shook as he ran it across his eyes. 'To make up for the lousy excuse of a father I was with Rad.'

Collapsing back into the chair, Pop seemed to have aged ten years.

'I was never around. The business consumed me. When I wasn't at the office I was schmoozing rock royalty, trying to woo the big names to sign with Landry Records. I thrived on a challenge and no star was too big or too small for me not to go after them.'

He shrugged. 'Rad never knew me.'

Speechless, Luca stared at the only man he'd ever trusted yet didn't really know at all.

'So you wanting to get to know me? That's been about *your* guilt?'

'Partly.'

Pop clasped his hands together to stop the shaking but at that moment, with his head reeling from the impact behind the truth, Luca couldn't dredge up pity.

'But it only took a few visits and I was smitten by every cheeky, rambunctious inch of you.'

The glimmer of tears in Pop's eyes hit him hard and he swallowed past the sudden lump in his throat.

'Accepting you, loving you, wasn't a product of my guilt. It was being charmed by a little boy who had so much to give without demanding anything in return. Then you grew up and didn't want much to do with me, just like your father, and I was so useless at bridging the gap, wanting to but still not having a clue how to do it…'

Hell, the lump in his throat grew and his chest ached with the effort not to cry.

Luca didn't know how long they sat there, Pop's declaration hanging in the air between them, but when he was confident he could speak without his voice shaking, he said, 'So Rad never knew how to be a dad?'

He hated having to ask, hated sounding so needy, but hearing Pop's confession opened the door to maybe forgiving his father, letting in a breath of fresh hope.

He finally understood. He'd had a similar fear, not

being able to connect with anyone, not being able to love because he didn't know how, not having seen it firsthand and, somehow, empathising with Rad eased his bitterness like nothing else could.

Pop nodded. 'That's right, son. I'd always know when your mother had tried to set up another meeting, for he'd get this dazed, confused expression for days. Like he wanted to reach out but didn't know how.'

'But he never once acknowledged me. He shut me out.'

'He just didn't know how.'

He only just caught Pop's murmured, 'I should know.'

'Oh, Pop.'

Luca stood and bent to give Pop a manly hug, the first time he'd ever embraced his grandfather.

'We both have a lot of learning to do but I'm willing to try if you are?'

'You bet.' Pop sniffled and he gave him a moment to compose himself before straightening.

'Thanks for telling me the truth.'

'Long overdue,' Pop said, his gruffness masking a world of regret. 'Now, before I bore you any further with an old man's ramblings, don't you have somewhere to be?'

Feeling lighter than he had in years, he held out his hand.

'Wish me luck.'

Pop shook his hand, pumping it as if the next few hours were a foregone conclusion.

'You don't need luck, son. Charli's as smitten as I was all those years ago.'

Wanting to leave on a light note, he winked. 'Must be that legendary Landry charm I inherited.'

'Must be.'

Pop's smile warmed his heart. 'Now, go get our girl.'

CHAPTER FOURTEEN

CHARLI had just stepped out of the shower when she heard what sounded like a hundred tap-dancing elephants pounding at her door. Elephants that wouldn't let up while she quickly wrapped a towel around her and tied it between her breasts.

If this was yet another late-night visit from the *über*-efficient receptionist at Landry Records she'd scream. Business could wait until morning, especially since she'd been starting work at the crack of dawn the past few days.

'If this can't wait 'til morning it better be good...'

The rest of her rant died on her lips as she opened the door to find the last man she expected to see.

Luca didn't speak. He didn't need to, his sexy smile saying it all as his gaze started at her toes and swept upwards, lingering on the towel.

She burned beneath his stare, her skin tingling from more than a hot shower.

'Am I the only one seeing the irony in this?'

Heck, when she'd envisaged talking to Luca again, it had been a civilised, prepared-for conversation over the phone. No way had she prepared for this.

'I thought you were going to call?'

'I did, you wouldn't answer, so I came back in-stead.'

As he crossed the threshold he added, 'For you.'

'Don't put yourself out or anything,' she muttered, closing the door and leaning against it, clutching her towel, which was in danger of seriously unravelling along with her wits.

Thankfully, he gave her space, waiting for her to come to him. Smart move, considering she couldn't stay propped against the door all night.

'You let me in, so I guess that's a start.'

'Luca, I—'

'I'm sorry for acting like a coward that last time.'

He raked a hand through his hair, the caramel spikes making her fingers itch to smooth them.

'I should've said a proper goodbye.'

With a sigh, she released the death-grip on her towel and eased away from the door.

'What was left to say?'

'Plenty.' He hesitated, and she'd never seen him so uncertain. 'I took the easy way out when I should've faced the truth.'

Confused, she bided her time, blown away by his appearing on her doorstep like this only days after he'd left but struggling to make sense of it.

The truth was she loved him and she'd made no effort to hide it their last night together. So maybe he'd finally realised; so what? It meant she had to deal with it and move on with her life.

'And the truth is—'

'Is there really any point to discussing this?'

The raw pain she'd managed to subdue over the past week exploded in her chest again, just as agonising, just as devastating as when he'd left, and she fisted her hands, willing it to subside before she crumpled.

Desperate for air, her chest heaved with the effort of breathing as she scrambled for the right words to make him leave before she blurted the truth: how much she wanted him to stay.

'Charli, the truth is—'

'The truth is I love you! I know it. You know it. So why rehash our little fling?'

The declaration burst out of her, past the lump in her throat, ripped from her in a frightening gush of honesty that left her shaking.

She wanted to choke back the rest but having the truth ripped from her only made her want to blurt more. 'But don't worry, I get it. You're here to apologise for the way you left, apology accepted, so you can forget I said all that and go. Besides, nothing could ever come of it. We lead separate lives on separate continents—'

Before she could finish he'd swept her into his arms and hugged her so tight she couldn't breathe.

When she finally inhaled, warm male and citrus lime and pure Luca filled her senses, richly evocative, highly addictive.

She could've stayed snuggled in his arms all night but what would be the point? They were over and if he thought he could do this every time he popped into town, he could think again.

She'd resigned herself to bumping into him on occasion through Hector, quite capable of the occasional polite greeting at the office. But having him turn up on her doorstep, expecting he could hug her and touch her and reopen the wound every time she saw him? No way.

Placing her palms on his chest, she pushed gently and eased off on the bear hug.

'Say it again.'

His eyes shone with an emotion that snatched her breath.

'Say what?'

'That you love me.'

She shook her head, wondering if water had stuck in her ears. Why on earth would he want her to say that?

Drained to the point of her legs giving way, she said, 'Look, Luca, I'm not sure why you're here but there's nothing you need to say. We had a great time while it lasted, let's leave it at that.'

'Let's not.'

She gaped as he spun away from her, rubbed the back of his neck where the muscles stood rigid.

'Damn, I'm making a mess of this again.'

When he spun back to face her, she clutched the back of the sofa for support at his wild-eyed expression.

'When I first ran without saying goodbye I talked myself into believing it was because I had commitments elsewhere. But that was a crock. I didn't know how to handle the emotional stuff. I've never learned.'

'Because of Rad?'

'Yeah.'

His shoulders sagged, and while she felt a twinge of sympathy, she wasn't buying his excuse completely. She heard the sincerity in his tone, saw the genuine fear in his face, and while they didn't have a future, now he'd opened the door to this little powwow she was going for broke. That way, she'd have no regrets she held back when she had the opportunity.

'As much as having Rad for a father sucked, I think you're using him as a cop-out.'

He visibly recoiled.

'I know what it's like, not having a role model. I never had a mum, not really. She basically tolerated me being around 'til I hit sixteen, then she turfed me out onto the streets.'

He paled. 'My God—'

'I've dealt with it, moved on.'

She watched the figures click into place. 'Sixteen? That's ten years ago, just after Rad's funeral when I left Melbourne…'

'Yeah, Hector was grieving after losing Rad and you. I was squatting in his shed, he found me, took me in, gave me everything.'

Pride darkened his eyes to midnight. 'Pop's amazing.'

'He is. So that thing about not having good role models? I'm in the same boat as you but you don't see me cowering in a corner.'

She started pacing, second-guessing the wisdom of unburdening herself but feeling darn good in the process.

'I was like you. Superficially dating, seeing people casually, knowing it wouldn't lead anywhere. My mum hurt me; I built a wall no one could breach. But Hector showed me it was okay to trust, then you came along and I took the biggest risk of my life.'

And lost. Though that wasn't the point. She'd taken the risk of loving him and, while it hurt like hell to lose him, she now knew she could do it.

His jaw sagged before he snapped it shut. 'What are you saying?'

'That letting you into my life, I fell in love for the first time, knowing you would never feel that way about me.'

If the air between them weren't crackling with the ever-present underlying tension she would've laughed at his stunned expression.

'I'm your first love?'

'Uh-huh. So now you know.'

She turned away so he wouldn't see the glimmer of tears, waited for the slam of the door, expecting him to run faster than he had last time.

When he grabbed her shoulders and spun her around, his wondrous expression surprised her more than the fact he'd stayed.

'I'm the only guy you've *ever* loved?'

'What do you want, a medal?'

His mouth opened and closed, his stunned expression giving way to male pride as he tilted her chin up to study her face.

'You're right about a lot of stuff but not all of it. That part about me not feeling that way about you?'

Her heart stalled as all the blood drained from her face.

'I do. Love you, that is.'

She blinked, sure she must've misheard him.

'I love you, Charli. It's why I came back. Why I want to stay, if you'll have me. We can date, hang out, chill, whatever, as long as you're willing to take another chance on an emotionally repressed guy hell-bent on making up for lost time.'

Her heart leapt at his declaration before reality slapped it back down.

Luca didn't commit. It was why he threw pots of money at his charities but never actually spent time with the kids there. He was like some philanthropic Robin Hood without the tights.

So while he said he wanted to give a relationship a

go, it wouldn't last. He'd want to do the right thing, to be the opposite of his father to prove he could.

But how long before he got tired of the regular nights in and dirty dishes in the sink and the same cranky partner who'd had a crappy day at work and just wanted to veg in front of the TV with a chick flick and a tub of choc-fudge ice cream?

Luca was a free spirit, the type of guy who couldn't be tied down for long, and no chance in hell would she let him into her life only to have him leave at some point in the future when the going got tough.

She wouldn't put herself through that. If it was hard letting him walk away now, knowing he loved her, it would be debilitating if she got in any deeper.

Stepping out of his embrace, she backed away.

'Charli? Say something.'

Heck, what could she say without driving a stake through both their hearts?

Anger tightened his mouth. 'Though maybe your silence says it all.'

He advanced on her and she shuffled backwards until her butt hit a chair, the anguish in his eyes tearing her apart.

'Don't you think after the upbringings we had, loving someone is the ultimate gamble? Yet here we both are, crazy about each other, owing it to ourselves to see this thing through. I'm willing to try. Are you?'

The tears she'd been battling couldn't be contained any longer, trickling down her cheeks as wave after wave of regret and sadness washed over her, leaving her wrung out.

Luca made a move to comfort her but she held up her hands, knowing she'd lose it completely if he took her in his arms.

She desperately wanted to believe him, wanted to let him into her heart and her life. But while he'd been a coward in running out of here last time, deep down, she was a coward too.

She'd resigned herself to not having him, had steeled herself for days now to function without falling apart every time the memory of his kiss, his caress, his touch, popped into her head. And she'd been doing just fine, until he strutted in here, devastating her all over again with his declaration.

Was she running scared? Scared of giving him another chance despite her false bravado taking a risk in the first place?

Maybe now wasn't the time to be making any hasty decisions. She had to think, something that was increasingly difficult on the maximum of two hours' snatched sleep a night she'd been getting since he left.

Her head ached with the effort of sorting through her feelings, his honesty and the mind-blowing possibility of a future she'd never dared imagine. For now, she needed time and space and a good night's sleep to clear her foggy head.

She swiped at her tears and took several steadying breaths to stop her voice wobbling like her tired legs.

'Let me think about it. I'm dead on my feet and really need some sleep.'

Incredulous, he reached out to her before thinking better of it and jamming his hands into his pockets. 'That's it?'

On the verge of passing out from fatigue, she shook her head to clear the fog.

'What do you mean?'

'Doesn't the fact I love you mean anything? The fact I want to give us a go?'

Increasingly fuzzy, she waved a hand as if shooing him away.

'You loving me is unexpected and crazy and the best thing I've ever heard. But this is complicated. You're a guy who needs freedom. You'll get bored. You're busy playing Robin Hood and I love my job and Hector's involved and I need to think…'

But Luca didn't give her time to think. He bundled her into his arms, determined to never let go.

'I can't lose you, Charli. Not again.'

He cradled her close and buried his nose in her neck, inhaling her sweet floral fragrance, wanting to stay here for ever.

For ever is a long time… Who would've thought he'd ever contemplate it yet in that moment, holding Charli close, he finally understood what had driven his mum all those years, why she'd put up with fragments of Rad's time, why she'd tolerated being on the fringe of his life and taking what she could get.

If she'd loved Rad half as much as he loved Charli, he got it. He'd do anything to be with Charli, now he just had to convince her that his feelings were genuine.

Releasing his death-grip on her, he cradled her face in his hands, the confusion in her eyes spurring him on. 'Let's clear up a few misconceptions. Freedom is over-rated. I'll never get bored being with you. The Robin Hood thing you'll have to explain to me. But listen up.'

He needed her to understand so she'd never have any reason to doubt him ever again.

'Loving you isn't a one-shot deal I'll tire of. It's about your quirky sense of humour and your obsession with dragons and your love of aniseed drops.'

He brushed a soft kiss on her cheek. 'It's about your

ability to bring out the best in me, your affection for Pop, your constant striving to be the best.'

This time, his kiss lingered longer, drifting closer to her mouth.

'It's about you being brilliant and beautiful inside and out and making me love you for no other reason than being you.'

He slanted a kiss across her lips, felt her lips part on a heartfelt sigh beneath his.

'It's about you making me feel like I can be emotionally invested in us. For ever.'

He didn't give her time to hesitate or question or second-guess. He kissed her with every ounce of pent-up emotion making him crazy inside, kissed her until they were both breathless.

'That charm sure comes in handy sometimes, huh?'

With love shining from her eyes, she cupped his cheek. 'A speech like that is guaranteed to go to a girl's head and make her do all sorts of crazy things.'

He grinned and leaned into her hand. 'Like?'

'Like saying she loves you madly, passionately, deeply. Like saying she'd like to spend for ever with you too.'

The lump of emotion in his throat he thought he'd dealt with at Hector's reappeared, much larger, much scarier. But with Charli holding onto him, basking in her love, what did he have to fear?

'The Robin Hood thing? You hang with the rich, raising money to give to the poor.'

A shadow flickered across her eyes, sending an arrow of fear through him. 'What's wrong?'

'You give a lot to the underprivileged, especially kids, right?'

'Yeah.'

Her hand caressed his cheek before sliding lower and resting on his chest, over his heart.

'Well, seeing as you're now committed to me, how about we really test your new-found emotional powers?'

'Huh?'

She smiled and that organ beneath her hand swelled with so much love he couldn't believe he was a newbie at this.

'Remember those poor kids we handed out free concert tickets to in the country towns?'

'Yeah.'

He had no idea where she was going with this but as long as she was in his arms, she could keep talking as long as she liked.

'Some of those kids are into music. They had guitar cases and sheet music and stuff. Wouldn't it be great if we could do something more for them than hand out free tickets or take them backstage?'

'Like?'

'What about opening a music school in Melbourne for kids who can't afford it? You can fund it with your Robin Hood ways and I'll help run it and I'm sure Hector could be cajoled into offering record deals and—'

'You're something else.'

He silenced her with a kiss, blown away by her generosity and warmth.

'The answer's yes, by the way. If I'm handing my heart to you for safekeeping, why not spread it round to a few needy kids too?'

She nudged him, hard, and he laughed.

'And while I'm opening my extremely fragile heart up to you and these kids, guess you should know Pop and I had our first real bonding experience and I'm including him in the love fest too.'

She kissed him in response. 'You're incredible.'

'Right back at you.'

His gaze dropped to the towel knotted between her breasts.

'You know what else is incredible? My mind-reading abilities. I'm going to do what you wanted to do the first time you saw me.'

Her lips twitched. 'What's that?'

'Lose the towel.'

'Wow, that's some ego. Who said I wanted you to lose the—?'

He kissed away her false protest and let his fingers do the rest.

As the towel tumbled to the floor and they lost themselves in the pleasure of the moment Luca silently vowed to stock their laundry with the best Egyptian cotton bath sheets money could buy.

After all, he had a lifetime of unknotting towels ahead of him.

EPILOGUE

One year later...

'You sure this racket is good for the baby?'

Charli tilted her head up to smile at Luca. 'If I'd known you'd be this overprotective I'd never have agreed to marry you.'

Sliding his arms tighter around her seven-month bulging belly, he nuzzled her neck.

'Keep telling yourself that, Mrs Petrelli. Because we both know you're so crazy for me you're putty in my hands.'

She elbowed him, enjoying his indignant oomph.

'Be quiet. This music is fabulous.'

Luca winced. 'Storm Varth is way past it.'

Swivelling in his arms, she patted his cheek and smiled sweetly.

'Jealous because you can't pull off the ripped leather pants and see-through black singlet look?'

'Jealous? Of *him*?'

Luca puffed up his chest just in case and they laughed, watching the aging rocker prance across the stage, belting out a classic medley from a decade before they were born.

She patted his chest and he promptly deflated, hugging

her closer while jerking his head towards a corner of the stage where a young rock group were poring over sheet music.

'It's cool that our first batch of graduates from the music school was the supporting act tonight.'

Standing on tiptoe, she kissed his cheek. 'Thanks to you.'

Bashful, he shrugged. 'Hey, it was your idea.'

'We make a great team.'

A signature Storm Varth guitar riff made him jump and she laughed.

'Pop's rapt with the turnout.'

'Yeah.'

She peeked around the curtain at Melbourne's largest outdoor arena, the crowd a mass of stomping, screaming fans for the fifth night in a row.

'And thanks to you, we've got Storm signed to release his next two CDs with us.'

His humble grin made her want to hug him for ever. 'Yeah, who knew I'd turn out to be a regular Robin Hood plus the best agent in the music business?'

Wrapping her arms around his neck, she stood on tiptoe to kiss him.

'I never had any doubt.'

'Thanks,' he murmured in her ear, trailing soft, swoon-worthy kisses along her jaw towards her mouth.

'Now how about we skip the rest of this gig and head home? I hear a new shipment of towels just arrived...'

Charli didn't need to be asked twice.

* * * * *

The series you love are now available in

LARGER PRINT!

The books are complete and unabridged—
printed in a larger type size to make it
easier on your eyes.

Harlequin *Romance*

From the Heart, For the Heart

Harlequin INTRIGUE

BREATHTAKING ROMANTIC SUSPENSE

Harlequin *Presents*

Seduction and Passion Guaranteed!

Harlequin *Super Romance*

Exciting, emotional, unexpected!

Try **LARGER PRINT** today!

Visit: www.ReaderService.com
Call: 1-800-873-8635

Harlequin

 A *Romance* FOR EVERY MOOD™

www.ReaderService.com

HLPDIRH

 HARLEQUIN® HISTORICAL
Where love is timeless

Imagine a time of chivalrous knights
and unconventional ladies,
roguish rakes and impetuous heiresses,
rugged cowboys and
spirited frontierswomen—
these rich and vivid tales
will capture your imagination!

HARLEQUIN HISTORICAL…
THEY'RE TOO GOOD TO MISS!